THE TOUCH
SYSTEM

THE TOUCH SYSTEM

Alejandra Costamagna

Translated from the Spanish by
Lisa Dillman

**TRANSIT
BOOKS**

Published by Transit Books
2301 Telegraph Avenue, Oakland, California 94612
www.transitbooks.org

Copyright Alejandra Costamagna © 2018
c/o Indent Literary Agency
www.indentagency.com

Translation copyright © Lisa Dillman, 2021

First published in English translation by Transit Books in 2021

ISBN: 978-1-945492-50-1 (paperback)
LIBRARY OF CONGRESS CONTROL NUMBER: 2021932612

DESIGN & TYPESETTING
Justin Carder

DISTRIBUTED BY
Consortium Book Sales & Distribution
(800) 283-3572 | cbsd.com

Printed in the United States of America

9 8 7 6 5 4 3 2 1

This project is supported in part by a grant from the National Endowment for the Arts.

For Miska, the bird of my sleepless nights
And Hebe, for so so much

And what monsters, our ancestors,
nothing but stories that drive children crazy.
MARÍA SONIA CRISTOFF

When we're happy our imagination is stronger; when we're un-
happy our memory works with greater vitality.
NATALIA GINZBURG

She won't read them, Agustín thinks. Chilenita won't read them. He just loaned her the last three books that Skinny Gariglio, his friend from typing class, loaned him: *The Evil Inheritance*, *Panic in Paradise*, and *Devil Children*. A loan on a loan. He has to give them back to Gariglio the next week or else pay for them, if he likes them. The girl's bored, Agustín thinks. Which is why he gives her books. She takes them offhandedly, the way you take cards in a round of scopa, like the ones she plays with her grandparents at night. She takes them with such composure, something Agustín finds incongruous given her age. She shouldn't spend so much time with Nélida in that room, so filled with exclamations. He knows that beneath his mother's silences lie roars that could deafen anyone. Even a girl. Even a foreigner. Plus, they shouldn't make her take siestas, or spend her summer vacations locked up with old folks. Just look at him, only going out once a week to typing class. Look at him, living in this cave, just typing away, not even going to the plaza. As if this, his life, were the delayed prolongation of some war. A safehouse, one of those prisons for lefties that people say are right around the corner. Agustín hears the rumors but doesn't feed them. And the girl isn't actually locked up, that would be an exaggeration. Sometimes she goes out with her

11

cousin Claudia and they climb trees, do girl things. You can tell she likes being here, with relatives who inhabit a place so different, Agustín imagines, from her own country. He's never been farther than Mar del Plata (and that was a long time ago, with his mother, back when they still left the house). The girl, on the other hand, comes and goes every year, Chile to Argentina, Argentina to Chile, overland. He's heard the story of Chilenita and her father so many times: the plains, searching for the tracks of a train that no longer runs as they head eastward, whirlwinds like mirages, stopping along the way to pee or stretch their legs, the mountains off in the distance, the ascent, how much longer, papá?, the longest tunnel in the world—almost as long as Chile, Agustín pictures the girl exaggerating as she spreads her arms wide, as though the longest thing in the world were a meter and a half, a country falling off the map—the wind like a furious animal at the summit, the flag with white star on blue background and blood red on one side, the mountainous curves, the descent, and finally his house. The girl has a name but he calls her *Chilenita*, little Chilean girl. She's his cousin's daughter and they both have the same last name, same initials even. She could be his little sister, he thinks, the sister he never had. Sometimes he wants to climb into his cousin's Citroën 2CV and take off with him and the girl, go to the other side. Bring his battery-powered radio and listen to Elvis Presley until their voices die out. Elvis's and all of theirs. A family on the lam together, disappearing, off human radars. Devils disguised as angels, taking off into a nameless sky, another galaxy. Chilenita saving him. Getting him out of there, opening doors, forcing him to cross the sea if necessary, telling him that those books are a lie, that real life is something else. But the girl is a girl and she can't change history.

IMAGINARY KEYBOARD DIVISION: The keyboard
is divided into two parts by an imaginary
lime. The letters on the left side of said
line are depressed with the fingers of the
left hand. and those on the right side
with the fingers of the write.

He's about to die, her father says. His cousin, the last living member of his clan, his only cousin, is dying on the other side of the Andes. He can't go to Campana, he says, please, will she go and be with Agustín on his deathbed. Stand in for him, he asks stubbing out his second cigarette of the day. If she says yes, her father says, he'll buy her a ticket today, give her money to cover expenses. Whatever she needs. And Ania needs whatever. Ever since she got fired from the school she needs whatever very much. Money, stability. Ever since she started walking dogs, taking care of cats, watering plants while occupants are away. Ever since she met Javier while doing that. No, that would be unfair. Ever since she can remember, more like. Ever since her mother died when she was two and not yet a fully formed person. Ever since Leonora turned up and her father started speaking another language. A language with no tongue, unintelligible to Ania. Ever since Leonora appeared and her father started getting lost on a map of his own, sending her out of orbit. Ania has stopped listening to the words streaming out of her father's mouth and dived headfirst into a cloud of pressing needs and obligations. Scenes that arrive as if blown in by the wind. The first time the school inspector called her into her office and lectured her for several minutes on discipline, on the need to train upstanding young people (that was the word she used, *upstanding*, and Ania pictured an army of children marching with backs erect, upstanding in body and spirit both, upstanding in speech, stiff and unbending as walls). She was to be stricter, the inspector demanded. Monitor her students' writing, not allow blunders like those on the last bulletin board display, which had stories with errors like "falkin" for falcon (or maybe for talking, who could be sure), "mermer" for murmur, "snell" for snail, "dennist" for dentist, and "howture" for who knows what. In the kid's story, the one that made the inspector's hair stand on end, an animal had howtured, and Ania reflected on the strange suggestiveness of the sound: a yowl or a howl that punctured the air. Truth be told, she found her students' linguistic inventiveness marvelous. She thought of words as having tucks and folds, being forever on the border between the flesh and the world. And yet the actual children themselves (people in general, but children in particular), she didn't really care for. If she let her imagination run wild, in fact, she could think of them as devils. Children, the children that were her students, sucked up every inch of her life. Still, it never even occurred to her to correct them or button their lips: to make those lively tongues, still free of the froth of adulthood, stand up straight. Sometimes she thought she didn't quite have the touch for relating to people, that a plant or animal was much more manageable than a human. She had only a cat, an orange ball of fur turned involuntary relative, and that was quite enough. Sometimes she thought she wasn't cut out for working. At least not at a school, not policing others' conduct. And then there was that other matter: Ania didn't know how to sleep. Over the years she'd forgotten how to sleep. Diazepam, zolpidem, zopiclone, she'd tried them all. She was always tired, yawning in the middle of conversations. You couldn't go around like that and be in charge of a class, teach anything. You need to have better sleep hygiene, people at school said. And she found the expression amusing. Pictured wiping a soapy sponge over her exhaustion, sweeping up her nightmares. What Ania really wanted was to retire by forty, but that was impossible. Maybe housesitting was her future, being a stand-in occupant. Slowly turning into the people she substituted. Taking on their habits, eating in their stead, petting their pets, masturbating in their bed. Learning their behavior, creating a manual for each case. That was how she'd met Javier: spending a night at his apartment, alone, charged with the care of a convalescent cat. Javier lived three blocks away, in a miniscule place. He'd contacted her through an ad she'd stuck up with a thumbtack at the neighborhood liquor store. *I pet-sit, walk dogs, water plants.* He called, told her it was urgent, said he was traveling that very night and had no one to take care of his sick cat. He was on antibiotics for a urinary infection—the cat. He left a set of keys with the doorman and instructions on how to administer the medicine. Total confidence, the man had. Or extreme affection for the animal. Ania liked that. She said goodbye to her orange cat and came to take care of a gray cat that at first took zero notice of her. He looked up at her the way you look at a stranger, barely raising your head, and then settled his languid body into the sofa. If Ania couldn't sleep in her own bed, no way was she going to be able to sleep in someone else's. She tried in vain. The zopiclone had zero effect. At four in the morning she got up and went to pet the cat. The animal looked at her from the same position on the sofa and let out a deformed meow. A mermer, she thought, a howture. At five o'clock she made coffee, at six she had a beer, at seven-thirty she ground up the antibiotic, dissolved it in water, sucked it into a syringe, opened the cat's mouth, and administered the medicine. Then she lay down next to him and managed to fall asleep. At ten-thirty in the morning she heard the sound of the key in the lock; she was terrified. She knew it was Javier, but she was terrified. Prolonged insomnia and the vestiges of hypnotic in her system probably made her loopy. Javier greeted her as if they'd known each other all their lives. And they drank coffee and he talked about his job at a printer's and she talked about getting fired from the school and her inadequate severance pay, her uncertain search, her terrible sleep, her desire to retire this very minute, the money she earned housesitting, cat sitting, dog sitting, plant sitting that wasn't enough, was never enough. She had to do something, she said. Her father cleared his throat, bringing her back. Suddenly the previous scenes vanished and the rasp of his croaky voice prevailed. Javier, their first conversation at his apartment, the start of something, all vanished. Now what she saw was her father, in the same old cafeteria, his third cigarette smoked and a say-yes face, a don't-let-me-down face. The face of someone asking a favor. Leonora is convalescing, she hears him say. She thinks that's what he said but she's not sure. He needs to stay here with her in Santiago. Plus, her children and grandchildren are visiting, up from the south, he continues as though reciting a litany. All that's missing is the holy spirit, Ania thinks, though she's never seen her father pray or cross himself. After all, the man continues, he's her husband, her family. He's referring to Leonora, naturally. Stepfamily, she wants to amend. Basic rules of cohabitation, daughter. Which manual is her father referring to? Anyway, she suspects that's not the real reason. When Agustín, the last member of the tribe, dies, that'll be the end of his history. The end of Campana. And her father doesn't have it in him to witness the end. Her grandparents, her great aunts and uncles, all her relatives over sixty, they're all gone: the end of the line over there on the other side. Claudia is still around, of course, but she doesn't live in Campana. Besides she's one of the tree's newer branches, like Ania, under forty. The truth is, Ania thinks, the man is unable to see Agustín in that state because he senses his own demise. We're going extinct, my girl, her father says in a tiny voice. And those five little words pierce her skin. In that moment, without saying so, she accepts the request.

UNIVERSAL KEYBOARD: the order and
distribution of letter son the keyboard
follows a basic logic, thats far more
important that it seem sat first glance.
The letters are not placed randomly but
in such a way that those most frequently
used in language are found in easy reach
of the most agile fingers, while the
more unusuyal ones are placed futher
off. This is an emornous advantage that
allows quicker and smoother movements.
Neverthesls, when the letters were laid
out on the universal keyboard, they paid
special attention to the Enlish language;
this explains why letters like A, E, C, D,
S, which are usex frequently in Spanish,
are on the left, while the ones used lsse,
like Ñ, K, J, H, are on the right.

Her father asked her to do two things that morning: stand in for him on the other side of the Andes, and come over that night for his birthday party. He knows she and Leonora can't stand each other, which is why he asked the way he did. Please, Ani, please. Whenever he wants to win her over he calls her Ani, as though that were the key, the secret code. Her father is so obvious sometimes. I'm practically an octogenarian he went on, as though strategic use of the diminutive weren't enough. Her father and Javier can't stand each other either, so he's the card Ani plays that night: take that, papi! Until Javier turned up in her life, she was so tired of the bird-in-heat courtship rituals, the dates and the way the men she went out with devolved into little boys, that she preferred to be alone. Better a cat than a boyfriend, than a child, a thousand times better. Javier was twenty-five years older. When she told her father, he said, oh, so you're looking for a grandfather rather than a husband. She wasn't looking for anyone, who did he think he was. At best she was looking for him, but she wasn't about to admit as much. So instead of insulting him, she said, nah, he was so youthful he hardly looked a day over fifty. Fifty per leg? he joked. And didn't even ask his name. Ania pictured him with Leonora that night, commenting on his daughter's latest. A guy who could be her father, her father would say, some sixty-year-old, can you imagine? Poor thing, Leonora would murmur. It was like Ania could hear the woman's phony lament in the distance. Poor who? Poor Ani? Poor elderly boyfriend who'd have to put up with all their comments? Poor motherfucking you, she pictured herself saying aloud. And maybe that was why, out of pride, she'd held on so long, and in the end grown attached to him or used to him or just opened up to him and now here she is with Javier, the man who could be her father but is her boyfriend, at the door of the building where the man who is her father lives.

At nine o'clock on the dot ring the intercom, announce arrival to the concierge, it's me, my father's daughter (don't mention Javier), take the elevator up, knock three times softly on the door. Out of the corner of her eye, catch the faces they make upon seeing them arrive together. Greet Leonora, inquire about her health to be polite. Don't listen to the reply. Seek alliances with the dog off in the corner, a white hair ball on his little blanket-bed. A miniature, practically a mouse, this animal she's walked five times in the past two weeks. A dog that helps her pay the rent. Pet him just to have something to do with her hands, touch his wet nose and let her hands be licked. Relinquish him to some devil-looking grandchild who ruffles the calm and attempts to earn the beast's affection. Retreat to Javier, remote inhabitant from another dimension. Traverse the cloud of smoke and kiss her father before he lights his thousandth cigarette of the day. Hand him his gift, the red silk scarf that he himself requested. Grab a handful of grapes from a bowl on the table, offer them to Javier. Put three grapes in her mouth and hardly even chew them. Think about the grape arbor in Campana, about her and her father cutting down clusters of grapes for their drives back to Chile. Now say she's going to the bathroom, walk into her father's office. Look at the shelves and walls lined with family photos. Search for herself but not appear in any of them. Stepkids, stepfamily: walls inhabited by a foreign genealogy. Offspring with ash-gray eyes and round noses, nothing like her. Not find herself there, not exist. Look around and find the *Great Encyclopedia of the World*. The volumes, as green and opaque as the past, that they sometimes stuck in the Citroën so Ania could entertain herself on the trip. Volume 18, page 196: *tilonorrinco*, the satin bowerbird: *Ptilonorhynchus violaceus*. Black and white photo of a small potbellied bird that resembles a sparrow making a nest. A bird that, according to the book, is known for the males' elaborate courtship of females. They woo their chosen mates by building bowers, which they decorate with piles of leaves and buds kept constantly fresh. The male birds spread their wings and offer the shimmer of their feathers, chests held high. This is how it all begins, the encyclopedia states. Look at the nest photos, art installations more than mere refuges. Remember by contrast the nests that she and Claudia used to find in the orange tree on Calle 9 de Julio. As cousins they'd climb the tree, sail through the branches like a couple of monkeys and come across little bundles of straw. No sophistication at all, those Campana birds. Sometimes there would be an egg or two. They knew they mustn't touch them, so they simply looked and then retraced their steps: branch, trunk, ground. Her father always said birds were solitary types, that they mustn't bother them. Once, though, Ania took one of the tiny eggs and, *crack*, it broke in her hand. She was alone, her cousin was in class at the time. She didn't tell anyone. Her hands all sticky, *crack*, the mama-bird hovering. She didn't know what to do. What a boob, they'd say. She knew they would. All thumbs, she was such a booby. Her vision clouded: her clumsiness had upset the mama-bird's instincts. Turn out the lights, she hears from the living room. Take a pencil from the desk and draw a circle around the picture of the bowerbird. Get the urge to rip out the page, but suddenly realize the voices are getting quieter, *crack*. Close the encyclopedia, put it back on the shelf and stop dredging up old memories. Now comes the cake and Ania walks straight onto the stage where, in the dark, her father is protagonist. Chest held high, wings spread. Ania walks straight to Javier, who is waiting for her in a corner as though taking her place in the periphery. Leonora's children and grandchildren look like dignitaries at a presidential gala. Even the dog has stood up. All stationed in their proper places, hands ready to clap. Lights out, candles lit. Blow: one, two, three, seventy-three.

The following day, fledge: cross the mountain, replace her father.

THE ITALIAN IMMIGRANT'S MANUAL (1913)

From "paese" to port of departure:

In the hours prior to boarding the ship I do not recommend locking yourself up in fear in the hotel room. But I do recommend that you not behave like a traveler, dragging your cases around and attracting the attention of the cavalieri d'industria who abound, particularly in maritime cities. Be cautious, avoid falling into the arms of a swindler, but do go for a walk through the city. This will be a lovely memento, a set of impressions you'll take along when you leave the motherland behind. Return to your hotel at nightfall to rest for the voyage and prepare to embark the following day.

They used to make the trip overland, inching over the Andes. In the beginning, Ania recalls, you couldn't travel through their mass. Machines had yet to drill the gorge and they had to travel patiently over the peaks. She remembers winding up the road in the Citroën, making their way to the summit, stopping for a few minutes to look out over the washed-out landscape they'd left behind and then begin the descent from Cristo Redentor to the other side of the Andes. She and her father, alone together, no interruptions. Sharing the feeling, though they never put it into words, that they were being swept along by an imperceptible current. Then the plains, the whirlwinds, the train tracks crossing the pampas in the distance. But never the train, only abandoned tracks and half-built crossing gates, as though locomotives were more a latent threat than a fact. A sound like an out-of-tune flute screeching in the background. Every three or four hours they'd stop to stretch their legs (both of them), smoke (her father) or pee behind a bush (her). Ania died of embarrassment if a truck went by and honked. They saw my bottom, she'd scream at her father. You'll never see those people again, who cares? What if we see them at the gas station? They won't recognize you . . . All butts looks alike, her father said. And to Ania, *butt* sounded cruder than *bottom,* the *u* tanned and hardened the word, gave it a strange magnitude. At the next gas station she would cover her head with the big bamboo hat that was always in the Citroën, so as not to be recognized. And when she was sure the honking trucker wasn't there, she'd get out of the Citroën and walk over to the cars parked further along. As her father filled the tank and took care of things, Ania would crouch before the cars' front grills to rescue trapped insects. The butterflies were always the most afflicted. To Ania they looked like miniature birds, birds with no song or feathers. She'd spread a scarf on the ground and line them up on it, one next to the other, with great care. She had to save them and get them flying before they forgot how to do it. The statistics were disheartening: only one or two of every ten could be saved. Her father had taught her that she mustn't graze their wings, mustn't get the little powder from their wings on her fingers, no matter what. If they lost that protective layer, that *cosmic dust,* he called it, it took their life. And she, surgeon of the songless birds, struggled to straighten their little legs, to reposition their singed antennae so they could take flight once more. Then her father would come and observe her makeshift hospital: the patients who were close to passing the test and those who would not make it. He'd light a cigarette and smoke, well away from the *smoking prohibited* area, as Ania finished tending to the last victims. Then they'd fledge once more (them: father and daughter) and look up and see that the clouds, gray and sticky, were losing their shape, becoming an ash-gray stain.

Clouds about to burst, stopped in their tracks by a thin line of sun.

The sky: floating, unstable fabric.

Agustín watches Chilenita put the novels he's just given her on the ground and climb up on a box to pinch grapes off a cluster so ripe it's about to explode. She says she doesn't like the grape skins so thick, says, in a Chilean way, that they gross her out. Says in Chile they're so thin you don't even notice them. She brings a grape to her mouth and sucks out the juice. Tosses the skin to the ground, right beside the books, mere centimeters from Agustín's feet. He's sitting on the green wooden floor, smoking, on the shared patio between the two homes. He can't tell if the girl is talking to herself or to him. Maybe in Chile little girls play like that. Agustín wonders if she has any type of boyfriend back home. Please, Tinito, she's just a girl. He can't picture her kissing anyone, she's his niece, his cousin's daughter. Agustín has never kissed a woman. Well, okay, his mother, but she doesn't count. Once Gariglio tried to teach him the tongue movements with his own mouth. He told him to open his lips slightly, like in surprise, not wide like to scream, and to close his eyes. Agustín felt the moist tip of something that seemed alive and dangerous. So he bit. But Gariglio bit back, and with their eyes open and tongues bleeding they spent several seconds tonguing each other's palates, the folds of their gums, their teeth. Gariglio had brought him a load of scary books, in case the girl was interested in any of them when she came for the summer. It was still a couple of months away, but Agustín wanted to take his time choosing. When he was with Gariglio, it was like the rest of the world disappeared. The silhouette of his father outside, sitting on a little bench, listening to a game on the radio, smoking. And his mother, in bed, enveloped in darkness. Not even the girl's grandparents or the girl herself (if she was visiting) in the house next door survived in his imagination. That day, when Gariglio tried to teach him the tongue movements, there was a silence so resounding that it forced them to listen to their own heavy breathing. If they'd paid closer attention they could have discerned the exact sound of the air entering their lungs and exiting their still-open mouths. His friend lit a cigarette and they shared it. Small dots of blood stained the filter, like the lipstick Nélida wore when she used to go out. You can't do anything, Gariglio said. It didn't sound like a reproach, though, more like resigned confirmation. The refrain from a waltz as old as friendship. Now Agustín is watching the girl out of the corner of his eye. He doesn't want her to know he's looking at her. He doesn't want her to leave. In an hour it will get dark and he'll go back to his cave and Chilenita will go to her grandparents' to play a hand of scopa or to keep reading *Panic in Paradise, Devil Children*, or *The Evil Inheritance*, if she even actually reads the novels he loans her. In the mornings, the girl tends to stay in the house. It's still December and her cousin Claudia is in school. Chilenita sometimes goes to meet her and they spend the afternoon together at their grandparents' house. But that's only sometimes. Most of the time, actually, the girl is alone or else locked up with Nélida in her darkened room. He should talk to her more, Agustín tells himself. Use the books as a way to approach and get her to tell him what it's like on the other side. Take him to her country, he wants to beg, though he'd never dare go that far. He should say it to her father, but how embarrassing. If his parents found out he's thinking about abandoning them, they'd never forgive him. Our whole lives locked up inside for you, our whole lives protecting you from the world and now here you are casting yourself into unknown lands, to foreign skies, and tossing us aside. You're a rotten son. What does it matter if they don't forgive him? It matters, Tinito, it does. He could write his mother a goodbye letter; take the typewriter that she herself gave him and say Enough, Nélida, the crystal is broken, I am no longer a little porcelain figurine. Children, weed, lightning. I myself am broken, Nélida, though no external force caught up to me. I broke my own self and now I'm leaving you. He knows that this would be a cluster bomb. One more bomb in Nélida's wayward head. A stick to the skull. He can't. Yes, he can, what do you mean you can't walk through that door, go across the city, walk or run or fly and leave this cell behind? Your mother did it, all the way from one side of the ocean to the other, at twenty-something. Your cousin, Chilenita's father, did it, he left his parents, his relatives, his country, and ran off to the other side of the Andes forever. But not him, not Nélida and Aroldo's only child. He doesn't have the character or the money or the skills. All he has is a typewriter he hasn't fully mastered, a radio to listen to whatever dramas, tangos, and gringo music he can tune in to, and a mountain of thoughts that disconcert him every day. Chilenita, though—her, he can still save. Or she can save him. Help him get out, even without moving from this little green floor on the shared patio. She's someone's child too, she knows. Don't let summer end, please, don't take the girl away.

EXERCISE 31

brave brave Brave brave brave brave brave
brave brave brave bravve brave brave brave
brave bbrave brave brave brave brave brave
brave brave brave brave brave brave brave
brave brave brave btave brave brave brave
vbrave brave brave brave brave brave brave
brave brapve brave brave brave brave brave

children childrenn children children
childrem children children hildren
children children children children.
children children children children
children Children children children
children children childreb children
children children children children
children children children children

caves caves caves. Caves caaves vaves
caves caves caves caves caves caves caves
caves caves caves caves caves caves caves
caves cavess caves caves caves caves caves
cabes caves caves caves cabes caves caves
caverm caves caves caves cavbes cavascaves
caves caves caves caves caves caves caves
caves caves caves caves caves caves caves

```
weeds weees weeds weeds wedds weeds
weeds weeds weeds weeds weeds weeds
weeds weeds weeds weeds weeds weeds
weeds weeds weeds weeds weeds weedeeds
wweeds weeds weeds weeds weeds weeds
weeds weeds weeds weeds wedsds weeds
weeds weeds weeds weeds sweeds weeds

Campana campana Campana Campaña Campana
Campana Campana campana Campana Campana
Ccampana campana Campana Campana Campana
Campana Campana Campana Campana Campaña
Campana camPana Campana Campana Campana
Cxmpana Campana Campana Campana  Campana
Campana Campana Campana Campana Campana
```

From the airport in the capital to the center of town. From the center of town to a local bus that takes her out into the province. Her life fits in a suitcase, everything she needs is there. Stepping off the Paraná Express, in Campana now, she has the sense she's entering unknown territory. She spent frequent spells of her childhood in this town, her father depositing her at her grandparents' house and returning to Chile or going who knows where, alone, only coming back for her a couple of months later. And now none of it seems familiar. The people, the people's voices, the streets with people in the half-light, the wind rustling tree leaves, the smell of burnt plastic rising from the factory chimneys and mixing with the winds coming off the Paraná, a few blocks from the train station. She hasn't set foot in Campana since Agustín's mother, Nélida, died. How long ago, she can't recall. An eternity, yesterday. She goes straight to the public hospital, the same place they once sewed her head up. Agustín is in a cot, eyes closed and mouth open. He's wearing a patient's gown. Dim light from a 25-watt bulb, cotton balls everywhere, a chair, a ceiling fan that barely stirs the air. In one corner, the burning ember of a mosquito coil and its penetrating smell. And on the wall, right in front of the bed, a small-screen TV with a lock on it and a sign explaining how much it costs to use. Seventeen pesos an hour. Ania has no idea of the local exchange rate. Is that expensive? Cheap? Do they always charge to watch television in public hospitals? Either way, no one's interested in watching TV. Through the window comes the reflection of another television in the room next door. If she cocks her ear she can make out a faint sound, just a slight buzz, that must be some reporter's voice. On the screen, she thinks she can make out two or three bodies on a seashore. The latest survivors from a shipwreck on the Mediterranean, she imagines. She moves her gaze from the window and looks out the corner of her eye at Agustín. Skeletal and yet puffy at the same time, his skin like a hot water bottle. Cheekbones jutting out, like in a bad drawing. Ania thinks, this is no longer her father's cousin. Nor is it anything like the image of Nélida's lifeless body. What she sees now is not exactly a person: a state of flux, an evaporation, some other thing, is what she sees now. And yet she cannot shake the image of Nélida. Against Ania's will, her great aunt imposes herself and won't leave, though other sights circulate before her eyes.

On one side of the bed is Claudia, who's come from the capital to bid their moribund uncle farewell. Through the window comes the regular song of cicadas. Her cousin greets her in hushed tones, as though outside sounds were of no consequence but words spoken inside the room might penetrate the terminal coma of the man dying before them. You want some maté? Claudia asks. Ania agrees. They hated maté, back then, when they were granddaughters. What are they now? Too bitter, but she doesn't say anything. A strange sense of guilt settles in. As though she were somehow responsible for the family going extinct. Her cousin wants to have kids, perpetuate the breed, procreate, leave a trace. She sees her clock ticking and laments: my train is pulling out, little cousin. Ania, on the other hand, has no desire to replicate herself in anyone, to save anyone. At best, perhaps rescue some wounded butterfly from a windscreen. The cousins talk about the years they spent as practicing grandchildren, about the games they played on the shared patio, about endless summers this side of the pampas, climbing the orange tree, that time she went to meet her after school, which time? When she got whacked in the head. Look, you can still see the stiches. Ania pulls her hair apart into two sections, where the scar is, so her cousin can see. I don't remember that, Ania. Look, right here . . . How can you not remember? This very hospital, coming into the emergency room. Agustín, they talk about him, and about Nélida, about those who are gone. About Nélida being admitted to this same place after swallowing a bottle of pills. About Nélida talking about her nine-year-old nephew, killed right in front of her when a grenade somebody had forgotten to deactivate exploded after the war. For a minute Ania thinks her cousin has snuck into her brain and found the woman's decomposed body. Or that their great aunt herself is with them and going to lecture them from her eternal corner. Maybe she'll down another bottle of pills and go back to sleep, die right in front of them, with her son Agustín. Swap her own senseless death for a perfectly lucid one, consciously abandoning this world so as to return, in the form of a shadow at least, to the place she never should have left. To embrace her father again, under the ground of the Piedmont hills. Maybe she'll forget why she came, and instead of spending time at reunions, Nélida will detonate a grenade at the cousins' feet. Or set fire to the two adjoining homes. Ania reflects that her thoughts are not entirely her own, that this horror story gushing out unbidden doesn't belong to her. Now her mind's eye sees the schoolchildren, in Santiago. The children safe, far away. The ones who called her señorita and followed her everywhere like little pigeons with no wings, no direction. Then the children vanish and Ania returns to the hospital room. To Nélida, in Claudia's memory, which she's sharing aloud. The woman's left leg, that's what Claudia's talking about now. Her leg, full of shards from the grenade explosion, remember? Ania pictures Nélida's nephew as one of her students, dying in her arms. The bomb went off at school and she, Ania, was unable to save him. Ania's ankle is bleeding and she thinks that the pinkish, almost transparent liquid leaking out might resuscitate the boy. She wipes his skin with her blood: señorita's blood on the body of the boy who is now a bird that opens its eyes and attempts to fly. But he can't, again he has no wings. Claudia is still talking. She doesn't realize Ania is fading in and out of the conversation, of her imagination. Her cousin lingers over Nélida's resemblance to Silvana Mangano, the star in all the movies that came to Campana in the fifties. Remember? Claudia asks again. How am I going to remember when I wasn't even born yet? I know, her cousin says, but don't you remember how everyone said she was the spitting image? People talked so much about Nélida back then. Her troubled head, they said, her misfortune. Claudia remembers one time she saw her on the patio, screaming that she was a dog, pulling at her clothes until she ripped them. A boy dog, Claudia says Nélida said, not a girl dog. It struck her. Why a boy dog and not a girl dog? And she scratched her skin till there was blood, such an ugly scene, little cousin. Ania remembers Nélida's hands clearly. The five fingers of her right hand, joined at the tips, making a little bowl of her upturned palm, the slight wagging of her hand that was also an exclamation point, a sign of not understanding these other people that were her family, her blood, but also her devastation. What is this bullshit? Why the hell did they send me to this damn place? That must be what Agustín's mother's hand wagging meant. Then the cousins talked about her Italianized Spanish. About the way she said *gwar* for war, *langawidge* for language, *oncless* for uncles. About her slightly squint-eyed look. Ania can't remember exactly when the woman who'd been wrenched from her home began losing herself in images of the *gwar*. Back then Ania didn't really have a grasp on the parameters of sanity. But she does remember that Nélida's thoughts came to life all by themselves, unbidden, the European conflict from a butchered Argentina that she didn't understand. She stopped coming out of her corner, the dark cavern that was her mind as well as her room on Calle 9 de Julio, the house connected to Ania and Claudia's grandparents' house. Two dwellings joined by a common patio with a grape arbor, black grapes with skin as thick as memory itself, gelatinous inside. Ania had lunch at one house and spent the afternoon at the other. She'd flee the siesta her grandparents arranged for her on a cot beside their double bed, all of them under the ceiling fan's wooden blades. The sound of this breeze-making contraption that might, at any moment, detach from the ceiling and slice their heads off with its hatchet blades, like what happened to the butterflies butchered by cars on the road. Ania ran from the torture of that siesta to take refuge next door with her great aunt, who barely ever left from her darkened room. She brewed maté for her, took her little cookies she stole from her grandparents' pantry and sat down to listen to her. Chile and Argentina were on the brink of war, the Argentines were winning the World Cup, old people were celebrating, in Campana there were three clandestine detention centers and, they said, even a "people's jail" where the guerillas meted out their own justice, but Nélida would talk about a war on the other side of the pond, the other side of memory. The cousins talked about that now too. About what it means to live separated by a mountain, by an ocean. About parents going extinct. About your mother, about my mother, who we don't name because they've been gone too long. About Leonora, who's Leonora? Oh, right, right, your father's wife. Oh, right, right, the southerner who won't let him travel. It's not that, exactly, the Chilean corrects. But you're the one who says so, the Argentine responds. Why else are you here, otherwise? Ania is about to say that it's not only that, that she came because she needed to breathe. But their conversation is cut off because at that exact moment Agustín sets off the motor of the poorly calibrated machine in his lungs. The cousins think this is it now, this time he's leaving them, and stand rooted to their spots. But five, ten, twenty minutes go by and his agonized breathing continues to accompany them. Miniscule breaths, but real ones. The man's turbines never shut down.

UPPERCASE: At the bottom oft he keyboard,
on either side, one can find special
keys which are used to create uppercase
letters. The proecdure is simple: pressing
one of the keys and holding it down,one
then taps the desired letter. On releasing
the key, then, letters typed will return
to lwoercase.

He should have done it years earlier, Agustín thinks. When
he found his mother in bed, staring vacantly, drool hanging
from her mouth, the empty bottle on the nightstand. When
Aroldo was delivering yeast to clients outside Campana.
When there was no one home and he had to call an ambulance
and help load her into it and watch them take her away and
pick a couple of oranges off the ground mechanically, just
to distract himself, and lock himself up in his bedroom to
type for the sake of typing, as if the typewriter keys were
bullets that could pierce his heart. Take the immigrants'
manual or some document from his mother's trunk and just
type. Strike something with his fingers, leave a trace, letters
like projectiles. Copy out fragments of his typing exam or
random words, as a last resort. Travelers, fury, brave,
dig. Then Aroldo returning, what happened to Nélida,
what did you do to your mother, then the hospitalization
and no visitors allowed and days alone with his father, the
airless house, the blinds drawn, the radio talking for no one,
the kitchen a desert, the metal maté straw their sole point
of contact, two ghosts with nobody to mourn, specters of
the present who don't even have a past to be proud of or a
future to come and herald, then in the end visit her in their
capacity as apparitions and discover that the woman's mind

has filled with fuzzy little hairs and they're devouring her; the fuzzy hairs are alive and hungry and mixing up her head, drawing her into a shell, and ultimately the outside world turns out to be far less dangerous, Tinito, than his mother's thoughts running wild. The doctor recommended they let her travel to Italy, go see her parents. It might cure her, he added with an unconvinced expression. Aroldo resisted, what if her roots swallowed her up and they couldn't get her back again. But in the end, he gave in. They sold furniture, borrowed money from relatives, indebted themselves to everyone until they'd collected enough to buy the plane ticket. Agustín noticed that, before she left, his mother regained some vim and vigor: she sewed herself two new little outfits, had her glasses repaired, even began to focus her gaze once more. And then she sent postcards from Italy, snapshots of herself with her parents, her sister, her brother-in-law, her nieces and nephews, the ones who were still alive (not a peep about the nephew killed before her eyes years ago). He should have written back, Agustín thinks, should have forced her to stay there. As your only child I compel you, I command you, I beg you not to return to this land that is not yours. Release her, that's what he should have done. A black and white image he cannot stop seeing: his mother with a guitar, smiling as if she were to be crowned the following day. On the back of the photo, a message in her perfect round calligraphy: "This is your mother, with short hair and a guitar. I've already listened to so many Elvis Presley records." She was smiling too wide, Agustín thinks, exaggerating new joy. As though there were no hard feelings. As though suddenly she'd decided to be reborn and not reproach anyone's conduct; become the person she was always meant to be. Not come to the

Americas, not marry, not have him, Agustín. The image pierced him like a stake through the heart. Nor can he erase the impression he got when he saw her return. She came back different: now she was a woman who'd seen her father. But it was just a type of break from her already damaged mind. After a few months, she got lost once more and sank deeper and deeper into a world only she could enter. His mother was no longer his mother and nobody could bring her back. Someone had taken her, Agustín realized at that moment. And it struck him that he was partially responsible. Perhaps his father hadn't been so wrong: what had he done? What the hell had he done to Nélida from the moment he was born? Maybe if he hadn't handed her over to the doctors that morning but to the captain of a ship to transport her out of Campana forever, downriver. Maybe if he'd planned a secret escape. But how was he going to do that when he couldn't even ride a scooter. He could have fled with her on Gariglio's bicycle: a son pedaling away, his mother on his back. Though maybe it wasn't him but Nélida's own father and mother who wrecked her head so many years ago. Sending her against her will to this land when she was barely twenty years old, practically forcing her to marry Aroldo, her second cousin, the only bachelor in the family. A young man, not too attractive, people said, but young and willing to marry the little girl who had his blood. Wanting to save her and instead damning her. Agustín now needs to talk this over with someone, but who? Someone please explain to him the root of her misfortune.

Acá yo con mi papá, Ricardo y Patrizia.

Yo, mi cuñado y Patrizia y Ricardo en el patio de San Rafaele. Estoy con delantal después de haber lavado los platos.

Yo y mi hermana en una pileta de natación. Mi cuñado estaba en el agua y sacó la foto. Te gusta? Ciau

They call them *bodies*. From one minute to the next they stop being people and become *bodies*.

Gaze into his pupils, unsure, rest a hand on a heart that no longer beats, confirm. Call the nurses, the guards on duty, the receptionist. Tell them it's all over. Look at Agustín's body for the last time, let them take him away. Sign documents.

As soon as the funeral is over, the most pressing matters dealt with, Claudia is going back to the capital, to her job and her old life. She's only come so Agustín wouldn't be alone on his deathbed. She opted to stay in a hotel in town rather than at the house on Calle 9 de Julio. More comfortable, she said. So she'd have a shower and a bed close to the hospital. But Ania knows that comfort alone is not what moved her. Or it is, but not in the way her cousin presents it. Both houses are now uninhabited, rotted with damp. Orphan abodes, no bodies to bring them back to life. Agustín was the last inhabitant, and he followed in his mother's footsteps and holed up in the same cave. The patio joining the two houses was slowly colonized by wild vegetation. The ground, a nest of leaves and smashed grapes. Something has to be done. Ania offers to stay a few days, do whatever's necessary to get things in order, and then begin arranging for the sale or demolition of the houses. Nobody really knows what to do with these two concrete skeletons. Though "nobody," at this precise moment, is the same as saying the granddaughters: the involuntary heirs. Ania's father is not about to get involved in any of it. Leonora is right there beside him to make sure of that. As far as he (or she) is concerned, they can donate the property to some foundation or to the neighbors or, if nothing else, to anyone who actually wants to live in that rusty old town. At seventy-three, her father needs to shift gears, he (or she) says, think about other things, look after his wife, his dog, stop mucking around with nonsense. In the end, the family properties are more a hassle than an inheritance.

Ania doesn't dare enter Agustín and Nélida's house, she's afraid of the spiders, the critters that have no doubt set up shop. The ghosts. She opts to stay at her grandparents' and put out feelers, get the lay of the land bit by bit. But where once there had been a semi-detached house, now all that's survived is an attic and a couple of inhabitable rooms, if a tile-floored space with a moldy ceiling and curtainless windows qualifies as *inhabitable*. On the lone side table is a black phone that looks fake. Ania picks up the receiver and is astonished to hear a dial tone, it works. On the wall opposite the phone is a row of family portraits. The one that stands out most is of Nélida: a full-body shot of a woman on a pier. The spitting image of Silvana Mangano, indeed. She's wearing a blue knee-length dress, a bone-colored leather coat and a hat with a veil covering her face. It's unclear if she is waving a final goodbye or a first hello to the people observing her, if she's about to embark or has just arrived in this land. In other photos are her grandparents, her great-grandparents, her great-aunts and uncles, Agustín. Some now faded by the nebula of time. Ania searches for herself without finding herself, she doesn't exist yet. She already doesn't exist, she corrects, she will never occupy this space. All dead, those pictured. All except for the boy with hair combed into a slightly ridiculous pompadour, sitting by a stuffed dog, who smiles precociously in one of the photos and will much later become her father. Ania takes the portrait and puts it face down on the phone table. She gazes out at the patio and sees rubble and the remains of a grape arbor and dust and gelatinous grapes on the ground and cicadas singing for nobody. She turns her gaze back inside the house and can just make out, at the back, the stairs up to the attic where she used to hide to read the novels Agustín lent her; he'd interrupt his day to come over to her grandparents' house and discuss murder mysteries and vampire stories with her. Up in the attic, she imagines, the spider webs are alive and well, thick as wool, how huge must their feet be to weave fabric like that, she wonders now, as she searches for a good place to leave her suitcase. She opens a closet and sees it there, in one corner, as though hiding: Agustín's typewriter, which he inherited from his mother. Ania takes it out and sets it on the table. It's full of dust, but undamaged. She doesn't dare type. If she does, it strikes her, the whole place might collapse.

Finally she stows her bags in one of the rooms, the one that was her father's when he was a boy. On a lone shelf, in among porcelain figurines and water and electric bills, two books she immediately recognizes peek out. Two volumes of the *Great Encyclopedia of the World*, which no doubt got left there after some trip she took with her father. They probably forgot them or decided to leave them in Campana because they were too heavy and the Citroën already too weighed down. Who knows. Inside the nightstand drawer are capless pens, a cardboard fan, mosquito repellent, a calendar from 1983, a metal maté straw, a deck of Spanish playing cards. The cards they played scopa with, she supposes. Ania feels oddly comforted, accompanied. It's as if she'd been conversing with all of the ages she once was. In the whole house only two lightbulbs and one faucet work: at least she's not going to die of thirst or darkness in this cave where she'll be staying for the hours to come. She needs to find out where she can get online. Seen like that, in this setting, the idea of trying to find an internet connection is comical. But Ania is sure there will be at least one booth in town where she can connect to the real world. Travel through a screen to reality, which she seems to have left behind. She needs to find a pharmacy, too, in case she doesn't have enough zopiclone. She takes from her suitcase the black sweatshirt she brought for Agustín's service. Now she sees that the sweatshirt is black, yes, but has white lettering on it: *Are you ready?,* it wonders in English. She puts it on inside out, the letters tickling her chest, and walks out of the house to bury her father's cousin. She thinks she's ready, though not entirely sure for what.

GREAT ENCYCLOPEDIA OF THE WORLD (1964),
VOL. 13, PAGE 892:

Nebula. *Cosmic matter covering an enormous amount of space that can take numerous forms. It is important to distinguish between "galactic nebulae" (which is found inside the Milky Way star system) and "extragalactic nebulae," which are either other galaxies, outside of our own, or parts of our own. Diffuse nebulae can be luminous or dark, and are made up of giant clouds of condensed gas (principally hydrogen) and cosmic dust. The largest luminous nebula visible to the naked eye (albeit somewhat difficult to see) is the Orion Nebula; one of the largest of the dark nebulae, perfectly visible in the southern skies, is called Coalsack; of the extragalactic nebulae, two of the most clearly visible are the Magellanic Clouds and the great Andromeda Nebula, which looks like a fuzzy star. These three objects are all galaxies.*

The sky this morning is a thick white bedsheet. That's how Agustín sees it. He stares out the window and has the urge to take flight, hurl himself skyward and just keep going until he can touch the cosmic dust. He's got the books in his hand, he doesn't know what to do with them. Chilenita gave him back *The Evil Inheritance* and *Panic in Paradise*, said those ones didn't interest her but she'd give *Devil Children* a try. Just when Gariglio promised him that for Christmas he'd give him two whole boxes of horror novels. Then the girl said she had to go meet her cousin at school and they were going to an ice cream parlor that afternoon to celebrate someone's birthday or maybe it was their name day, Agustín didn't retain the exact information. But that didn't end up happening, there was no celebrating, because right after lunch, Aroldo decided he'd put her on the back seat of the bike, just go for a little ride around the block, him and his great niece, and she stuck her left foot on the wheel —always such a booby, Chilenita—and the spokes burned the skin off her heel and she was bleeding and screaming and the blood he saw coming out the girl's foot was all pinkish. And Agustín wanted to lick that skin, drop by drop. Help stop the bleeding, put his mouth on that warm blood and soothe her in a way that perhaps nobody ever had. Agustín was watching the scene unfold from his bedroom window, hiding behind the curtain, listlessly exhaling the smoke from his cigarette, unable to move a muscle. It was like a movie, playing out before his eyes. But the incident went no further. Her grandmother treated the girl's foot with alcohol and put on a bandage. That was it. Agustín thinks he shouldn't be thinking about her so much. Thinks he should keep his mind on his own affairs. But what are his affairs? Applying for the typist position at the pipe factory. Working with his father in the yeast business. Other affairs would be trying a hand at something totally unexpected. What if he offered his services as a hostage caretaker in some safehouse. He doesn't fully grasp who's who in that racket, but his sense is that it doesn't really matter. He'd need to find a contact, that much he's certain of, someone trusted, to get him an in. Maybe Gariglio knows someone. He could tell them his cousin, Chilenita's father, is a total leftie. That's what people say. That would be a great in. Taking care of hostages is something he'd be really good at, he thinks. More than think it, he's certain. He's a patient man, and screaming doesn't bother him. He's got nerves of steel, unlike his mother. On the surface he seems fragile as porcelain, but that's just appearance. His thoughts spin off farther and farther, and there comes a point when he can't or doesn't dare translate them into words. He tries to focus his gaze out the window, concentrate on the harmonious white sky. Impossible. He doesn't really know how to interpret what his head is ordering him to think right this instant.

Dear Sirs:
With regards to your advertisment in "La
Prensa," I would like to be considered
a candidate for the typist position. At
present I am employed as a typost, but
out of desire to advance my career, have
been styding shorthand at night and at
present am about to complete the course.
I take dictation at 80 words per minute
and expect to graduatr within a week. I
am 26 years old. You will be interestd to
hear that, to train for taking dictation
qu8ckly, for the past three weeks I have
attended various conferences in order
to transcribe talks, thereby obtaining
valuable pactice. I thank you in advance
for your consideration of my application
and offer you my kindset regards.

My second death, Ania thinks as she's walking toward the church. Agustín is the second person in her life she's seen lifeless. The first was Nélida, also in this place, years earlier. Ania thought at the time that mountains were just geographical accidents, physical walls and nothing more. Her grandparents, her aunts and uncles, a whole slew of folks had died: the family was disintegrating at top speed. Her father had yet to meet Leonora. So Ania traveled with him to the burial. They flew together, like a couple of convicts on a weekend's provisional release, out to inhale their freedom. Or equally secret lovers, with a funereal excuse not to leave one another's side. The degree of fear she felt at flying was infinitely smaller than that of the joy she felt at spending a weekend with her father on the other side of the Andes. When they arrived they were greeted like ambassadors. Holding hands, like the fugitive couple they were, they approached the casket, and that was her first sight of death. She had never seen her grandparents dead, her mother either. They'd died and simply vanished, that was it. Her child's brain had forgotten them easily, because to her the corpses didn't exist. But with Nélida it was different. That time she stood before the coffin and put her face up to the glass, almost touching it. She no longer resembled the frightened figure Ania remembered from childhood summers, when her father would deposit her in Campana to spend her vacations with family. Even back then her grandparents didn't have much time left, just a few ragged years, and by then Nélida's head was already off elsewhere. They lived in side-by-side houses: her grandparents in one; Agustín and her great aunt and uncle in the other. Ania would bring them little tins of seafood as gifts and Nélida would pierce the cans listlessly, using a gunky but still sharp opener, and pull out the clams or mussels one by one, her fingers like pincers, professional typist's fingers, fingers that had worked at an important factory in Italy, a two-story factory, people said, right up until her parents shipped her off to relatives, nobody knew exactly why, in the Americas. As they ate shellfish in the kitchen, her uncle would turn the volume up on the radio and shout "Goooooooooooal, Atlanta!" every little while, since back then the Villa Crespo team, which one of his yeast customers played for, used to win. And Agustín, always there in the background like a cardboard cutout: holed up in his room or smoking in the doorway of the house on Calle 9 de Julio with Skinny Gariglio, his only friend, dealer of ghost stories and cigarettes, a pale kid who went everywhere by bike. Ania recalls now, now that Agustín is gone and she has to say goodbye, the few conversations she had with him, his eyes stuttering and yet watchful at the same time, as if they didn't speak the same language but formed part of the same tribe. Nélida and Aroldo's son like a slippery patch on the path of her memories.

When Ania gets to the church she can't see Claudia. She thinks she's at the wrong wake. Ania imagines that these women wearing floral dresses in shades of gray (the same color as Leonora's eyes; what's Leonora doing here?) are local wailers, working for the city on commission, there to lend some atmosphere to town funerals. She thinks that she too has been hired by authorities and should kneel down in some corner and commence. Join her hands, lower her gaze and donate tears to an unknown corpse. Take the place of others, out of habit. Like at her father's birthday: attending someone else's ceremony. Pretend that joy or sorrow are pumping through her veins. Ania's thoughts are a bit scattered and memories come to her unbidden. It was two or three weeks ago, before she received the bad news about Agustín and knew she'd be coming to Campana. The phone rang one night, and on the tiny screen she saw "papá." She's always hated phone calls. Ania picked up on the fourth ring. "Daughter, I'm going to be a father," her father said. Just like that. And she, rather than congratulate him, felt she should offer condolences. Or rather, condole herself. She wanted to say, "But you're seventy-something, papá, and Leonora's no spring chicken." Instead she fell silent. And after a few seconds, her father broke the ice: "It's a Yorkshire terrier, but he looks like a rat." Anybody else would have laughed. But she's not anybody else; she's her father's only daughter. So it made her want to walk into a church and join any old bereaved person who might be there mourning a death, any old death. That night she needed the protection of every god, the inexistent and the imaginary. She didn't know why but she needed protection. The thing is she didn't believe in protective gods, nor did she believe that churches were open at night. And therefore, instead she said, oh, that's nice, do you want me to walk it? Her father knew that this human daughter was in need of money, and that was part of the reason for his call. It was a flat-out job offer. Without further ado they negotiated the fee Ania would receive for walking the dog three times a week. When she hung up the phone, she stroked the cat, put on a vest and went to the diner on the corner. She liked to imagine that the cat was her father's grandchild, but never told him so directly. If she'd had a garden, or at least a balcony, she'd have sat down on a lounge chair and downed a whisky, knocked it back straight, following the creeper winding along the back wall with her gaze. Since that was impossible, she sat at the counter and asked for a very cold beer, with foam. Then it dawned on her that she hadn't asked her father the dog's name. Bah, it was a dog. After all, her father hadn't asked her her boyfriend's name the first time she told him about Javier either. The one she should ignore was Leonora, not some little doggie who'd come to fill who knows what hole. After her second beer, she considered calling Javier. More than consider it, she did call him. But his voicemail picked up and she didn't want to leave a message. What could she say? Hey, Javi. My dad got a rat dog. What else was she going to do? Howl? Better to down her last beer and forget about her father and the dog and Javier.

Claudia is now waving to her from the back. Ania approaches and her cousin introduces her: Coletti's daughter, she says. Chilenita, the little Chilean. And everyone understands. As if there had never been another Coletti in town. As if the deceased himself and the rest of the family were appendages to her father. Señor Coletti, from Chile. The daughter of Señor Coletti, the one who turned Chilean. The Campana man who one day flew the coop and settled in a country with the name of a pepper. As if saying Chile defined everything, set some type of precedent. Ania submits to greetings, embraces, condolences. She feels like she's the only mourner in all the world, and has been charged with

58

holding vigil for the only deceased person in the universe. One with her last name and her blood. Claudia absolves herself from her responsibility and leaves Ania as sole decoy for all condolences. The foreign niece has more gravitas than the local. Chile one, Argentina zero. The provinces are all yours, cousin, my affairs are elsewhere. And no, Ania realizes now, she's not ready for this. She gets the urge to show everyone the writing on her sweatshirt and poll those in attendance: alright, let's see—who's ready? There isn't a crowd, but Ania feels overwhelmed. She doesn't know exactly who she is, who she should be in this situation. Stand in for her father, but how? Thank you, oh, thank you so much. She doesn't know what else to say, doesn't have the touch for this kind of situation. There are lots of faces that resemble Nélida, though none with the absent expression she wore when Ania saw her for the last time. She needs to concentrate on her assigned role, be master of ceremonies, to master a course she didn't choose to teach. She imagines the relatives gathered as children from her school and wants to disorganize them, smash the syntax of mourning that's withering their faces. Make them mermer, let them howture their hearts out. She tries to tune out, and in the effort her father appears. She and her father at Nélida's funeral, in a past that, examined from up close, resembles an uncertain future. The two of them, immortal, holding vigil over some other deceased. Leonora? Her mother? Suddenly it's she herself in the coffin and her father holding vigil for her. Nélida, Agustín, Aroldo, Claudia, Javier, who crossed the Andes expressly to be by her side, the fake-tears women, the whole town bidding her farewell. The scene makes her secretly happy, and without intending to she smiles while shaking hands and almost laughs out loud but manages to contain herself. Until a very thin man appears, a skeletal figure who gives her his hand and introduces himself. You probably don't remember me, he says.

In *Devil Children*, two siblings, a brother and sister, need fire in order to breathe. They need flames to oxygenate their lungs. At first they burn trash at some dump and use that to nourish themselves. But in time they discover it's not hard to short-circuit old houses and begin causing fires in the center of town. Flames everywhere, a city ablaze. Fire reaches the pyro kids' neighborhood, their house, their bedrooms. The curtains burn, the furniture, the walls collapse, their parents suffocate. And the siblings celebrate with diabolical laughter while struggling to breathe and watching their bodies melt before one another like a pair of rubber dolls.

"Ay, Aurora, you've thrown me to abandon. / The one who loved and loved you so." Agustín listens to the plaintive voice coming from the transistor radio. He likes to think the song is coming from his own mouth, his tongue of fire. "Punish her, oh Lord, with all of your might. / Let her suffer so, but never die." He likes to picture himself spiteful and vindictive. Let her suffer, but not die, the wretch. Who? Who cares, as long as she suffers. He takes the cover off the typewriter, invents a verse: "That old momma cat finally went and had a kitten." It seems totally nonsensical but he keeps going: "And though you don't deserve it, I'm still smitten." Skinny Gariglio will later tell him, as they're walking together, late to typing class, that the song is a waltz based on a Peruvian poem and not by Carlos Gardel, the way everyone thinks. What do you mean, it's not Gardel? It's not. Yes it is. Gariglio says people say Gardel copied it on a visit to Chile. But Chile's not Peru. Same thing, Gariglio says. The mountain and its shadow, same difference. What does Skinny Gariglio know about Chile? And who is this "people" anyway? But Gariglio never tells him who the people informing him are, the people who tell him things. Punish him, Lord, with all your might, Agustín murmurs before beginning to type. Let him suffer so, but never die. The rest of the chorus runs like a fine-tuned train.

She saw the bike at the entrance to the church, and now, as he stands there before her, connects her memory to his presence. She knows it's Skinny Gariglio. A boatload of years have gone by since the last time she saw him, at Nélida's funeral, but he's not hard to recognize. Something about his figure makes her uncomfortable, something incomplete that she soon hits upon. Gariglio looks like he's lugging Agustín's shadow around. It's impossible to see him as an autonomous person, her memory thwarts the attempt. She never bumped into him alone: not in the plaza not on the street with all the ice cream parlors not at Campana train station. Gariglio would appear with Agustín, down Calle 9 de Julio, his bike on one side and all his little horror books in a bag. Ania would spy on them from the attic balcony at her grandparents' to assess the consignment. She knew that Agustín would knock on the door later, ask for her and show her the books he'd selected using who knew what criteria. Ania would watch him, listen to him stutter, think that if the man had a tail he'd hide it between his legs. He was that timid. She would then take the books, more out of kindness than genuine interest, and at night, after a round of scopa with her grandparents, back in the attic, once the old people were snoring and the cicadas silent, fanning herself with the cardboard fan, she'd lose herself in the novels' tempestuous tales. And that's how it was, so many other times: Agustín and Gariglio, always together, with the books, with the bike.

And yet Skinny Gariglio is now but a slip of the man she recalls. His bones have sucked up his skin and he's got almost no hair. He wears a beret that hides his baldness but doesn't entirely conceal it. The man holds out his hand in excessive deference and takes off his beret as a sign of respect. Of course I remember, Ania says. And their dialogue falters. I'm so sorry, Gariglio adds. For a second she forgets the context, the wake, and doesn't know what he's so sorry about, this guy standing before her. Is he so sorry about the silence oppressing them? Is he so sorry to be standing before a person who seems a bit out of it? Ania glances at Agustín's casket, at the people all around, cousin Claudia in the back, and quickly orders her thoughts. We'll all be going there some day, she responds, as if attempting to escape the role of condolence-receiver, of stand-in for her father and, now, her cousin too. Maybe they should switch roles, she thinks. Gariglio is much more grief-stricken over Agustín than she is, after all. Everyone else at this wake, including her and her cousin, is a minor character. The only one who should matter here is Skinny Gariglio, Agustín's best friend, his shadow. She feels like giving him her hand and saying that she, too, is so sorry, that Agustín must be at peace now, God has a plan. She has the urge to repeat all the platitudes and phrases she's heard over the past few hours and that, obviously, she doesn't believe. But suddenly she imagines the man breaking protocol, taking a book printed on copier paper from his bag and beginning to read from one of the little novels he used to traffic. *Panic in Paradise* and an overarching silence. And Agustín busting out of his coffin and emerging with his pimply living-dead face and a diabolical laugh and all of the dead coming to life and the mourners all running for shelter, terrified, and Gariglio closing the book, amen. Ania understands that this is her way of saying goodbye and, at the same time, fleeing from all the aggrieved relatives: the close ones and those lost in history. The ones she never met, even. Fleeing from their uprooted customs and hushed tones. Suddenly she realizes that Gariglio is waiting for her to say something in reply, but she doesn't know what he asked. When is she going back to Chile, the man repeats. Ania thinks about the cat, her father, Javier. Her father's dog, the houses she committed to sitting the following week, the odd jobs that might crop up and that she desperately needs. She should go back tomorrow. Forget the paperwork, forget these ruins, forget Agustín, forget Nélida, and go back to her world. Forget this nonsense. But she just arrived, she can't give up so soon. She's not sure of her return date, she says. Where can she get online, she asks. To her surprise, Skinny Gariglio knows where. An internet café in town, run by a Uruguayan couple, they have booths where people can make phone calls and one computer. A couple blocks from Cecil's, he says. And he jots down the address on a crumpled scrap of paper he pulls from his pocket. He's got a pencil tucked behind his left ear: a self-defense weapon, Ania thinks. If he's attacked, he's got a tool ready to bury into his assailant's eyes. Gariglio's writing is coarse, big bold characters that more resemble squiggles than anything else. He sticks the pencil back in place, then changes sides, tucking it behind his right ear instead. Then he clears his throat and says that he can lend a hand getting the houses in order, if she needs help. Ania acknowledges his kind offer without much enthusiasm. She sends him off with the same extended hand as before, this time in farewell. There are several more condolences to receive.

As they are being consumed by flames, the boy opens his mouth and, rather than stick out a tongue of fire, as might be expected, he squawks. The girl tries to do the same, but she no longer has vocal cords to make sounds. The two of them are shadows of themselves. Up above, in the sky, a flock of smoldering sparrows disappears into twilight's pallor. What follows is something like silence, something the same shade of orange as the birds. A disembodied voice. Down below, on earth, the children have lost their human form. But if we cock our eyes, we can make out a shape moving in the embers. The story of the devil children might not end with the last sentence.

Somebody has to warn her. Agustín heard it on his way back from class. We should beat that chick with a fucking stick: he heard it clear as day. Maybe the boys were kidding and he's taking it too seriously. But he should tell somebody: the girl herself, some local official, Gariglio. Not his parents, no way. They'd isolate him even more, forbid him from going anywhere near the kids at school. Maybe even isolate him from the girl. Various scenarios run through his mind on fast forward. Thoughts like rocks. Agustín has a hard time knowing when people are being serious and when they're joking. But theirs are not friendly nations these days, that much everyone knows. Take her into a corner and feel her up head to toe, coast to coast, so she sees what happens when you mess with the motherland. He can hear the uppercase they use to pronounce the word Motherland. You can't lay a finger on other people's country without paying the price, who does that stupid chick think she is? That's what he heard at the school entrance when he was coming out of typing class. Gariglio had left early because he had a dentist appointment. So Agustín walked home alone. To other people, he doesn't exist, he knows that. People think he's an odd bird, like a kid who goes to all the after-school programs, an insignificance, less than a man. Skinny Gariglio commands respect because he traffics in books, he rides a bike. But not him. School is a dangerous place, Agustín thinks. For the first time, he thinks his mother is right; she pulled him out of school so he could be taught at home. To avoid outside threats: the world is a very dangerous place, Tinito. And then he started being left out, losing friends. He had a hard time forming relationships with people his age. He didn't know how to approach people, what to talk about. Though it doesn't necessarily seem to be a question of age. With Gariglio everything is different, because his friend doesn't differentiate. Agustín can talk about almost anything with him. About people's general scorn, for example. About horror stories and their possible ties to this world of blood and bone. Those are things he can always always talk about.

In the end, he asked Gariglio to extend his loan on *Devil Children*. It seemed like such a shame for Chilenita not to finish the book. He was afraid of no longer having a reason to knock on his grandparents' door, of having to settle for bumping into her by chance, as if he got that many chances. Gariglio told him to keep all three books another week, so he could read *The Evil Inheritance* and *Panic in Paradise* too. One was like the continuation of the other and he was going to like them, he *had* to like them. He told him again about the boxes of books he was going to give him at Christmas. And loaned him two more books, vampire stories. He doesn't like those as much, but he wasn't about to turn them down. Vampires are like trainees to something he doesn't know how to name. It's not "evil," he doesn't like such big words. Agustín doesn't know the exact word. He likes testing out words that might approximate whatever he's trying to say. Likes it but it also drives him crazy, never being able to come up with those words. That's why he types all the time, no rest and no rules: in case what he's looking for appears of its own accord, the word that will either bring him back or send him away forever. He knows the girl's father is coming for her in five days. He doesn't want her to leave, but doesn't want her to stay and be in danger either. He has to do something, has to save her.

The minute his parents turn out the light in the next room, he takes the cover off the typewriter and gets into the proper position. One day, he thinks, he's going to teach Chilenita to type. She's got elegant fingers, no doubt she'll perform this type of task well. Like his mother, when she still had her wits and her youth about her. When she was Italian. And they'll spend all afternoon together, keystroke after keystroke, him dictating and her typing away.

lightening lightning lightening lightening
lightning lightning lightening lightening
lightning lighnting lightning lightning
lightening lightening lightning lightning
lightening lightning lightning lightening
lightning lightning lighttning lightning
lightening lightning lightning lightning

fury fury furry fur fur6 fury fury fry fury
fur fury fury fury fury furyfury fur fury
fury fury fur fury fury fury fur fury fury
fury Fury fury fury fury fury fury fury fur
fury fury fury fury fury furyfury fury fury
fury fury fury fury fury fury fuyry fury
fury fUry fury fury fury fury fury fury

travelers traveles travelers travelers
trvelers traveler traveldrs travelers
travelers travelers travlees travellers
travelers travellrs travlers traveler
travelers travelers traveles travelers
travelers travelers traveler travelers
travelets travelers traveler travelers

flag flag flagflag flag flag flag flag
flag flag flag glag flag flag flag flag
flag flag flag flag flag flag flag flag
flag flag flag flag flag flag flag flagg
fvlag flag flag flag flag flag flag flaag
flag flag flag flag flag flag flag flag
flag flag flag flag flag flag flag flag

children children chilildren children
children children children children
children childrenn childr en children
children children children children
children children children children
childrenn children children children
children childrn childrenchildren

Ania accompanies Claudia to the entrance of the hotel. They walk silently, as though floating on their own surface, each on a separate one. They say goodbye with a hug that conveys relief more than it does sadness. Claudia will put the properties' notice of sale in the Campana paper, and the capital paper too. Just in case. And she'll phone to keep tabs on things. If you start going kooky, just shout, her cousin says. Though she's being serious, the sentence makes Ania laugh. The expression makes her laugh. Going kooky. Like she's a bird or a crazy person. A cuckoo. She knows she's going to have trouble getting to sleep, after the funeral there's too much noise in her head. She decides to go for a walk to shake off her thoughts, or at least settle them down. But the funeral wasn't the only thing that messed with her head. She doesn't know where exactly these involuntary images are coming from, the ones surfacing right now; the change of scenery, she supposes.

In the plaza, right beside a jacaranda in full bloom, is a monument to immigrants. It wasn't there last time she came, she doesn't think. It's a dark stone with ten words painted in red letters, "Like a wave behind the ocean from Italy to Campana." Ania thinks of those surging tides of pride and exile. Everyone searching for America, for the promised land, following some relative who promised riches on this side of the world. They disembarked in the hopes of making fast money, but before long their fortune became survival and America a hostile territory. The oceans of grass and infinitely fertile fields and the land they'd been promised didn't exist. Soon they had to learn to be others. Work at anything, send money to family, build new lives: that was the stuff of their days. And they were already there, they couldn't go back. Following no clear path, she walks to the train station. The platform is empty, abandoned. Further on she can see the riverbank, but her legs now take her in another direction. She goes back down the street with the ice cream parlors, walks past Cecil's, the bar that was probably born right along with the town, once more traverses the plaza full of old folks who now seem to be whispering shrilly, as if their vocal chords had been altered or they were imitating birdsong, and keeps heading left. At some point she realizes she's in front of the public school. It's closed, looks dead. She gets the sense that children no longer exist, they've suddenly grown up or gone off to follow their own choreography: holding on to one another's smocks, single file. She likes that idea: a child-free town. Leaving the school behind she walks slowly down San Martín to Calle 9 de Julio. In front of her grandparents' house she picks up an orange from the ground and peels it. Her hands get all bitter, the fruit is inedible. She leaves it there like a juicy pointless corpse.

Suddenly she thinks she sees Nélida across the street. What is the matter with you, Ania? Who's sending you these visions? Then she gets a stabbing pain in the back of her neck: someone poking her with a pin and extracting it very slowly to prolong the effect. She closes her eyes, but Nélida is still there. She realizes, without warning, that the woman has taken root inside her and now she's surfacing. And as she thinks this, Ania also thinks that she very much likes the expression *to take root*. A strange and beautiful image. As though memories were first planted, then sprouted from pores, *crack*, with shoots, buds and thorns. Breathe, that's what she needs to do. Relax, empty her mind. Although perhaps the word is not breathe or relax but roost. It will do her good to spend a few nights in this place, she tells herself, far from it all. If the circumstances are right, she could even build herself a little bowerbird nest, fashioned like a work of art, and dwell in it until next spring. Spread her wings and take a test flight in these adopted climes. Though it's true that, according to the encyclopedia, those birds take such pains with their nests almost entirely to woo their mate. But no need to interpret everything down to the letter, Ani, she chides herself. Gets angry with herself, almost. Just make a butterfly nest and be done with it. Her father said if she needed more money to tell him. Tomorrow she can send him an email and explain the situation. There's the cat, yes, but Javier offered to take care of him. And he's exceedingly given to affection, the cat is; he clings to memories of an ancient kingdom and allows anyone to feel him up. Ania has no plants, no yard, no roots on the other side. As a last resort, she thinks, she could ask Javier to move up his vacation from the print shop, bring her the cat and stay with her a spell.

That night she takes a zopiclone and sleeps in her father's bed. The same room, the same bed her father slept in when he was a boy. Against all odds, she falls asleep immediately, effortlessly. But she doesn't dream. The moment she wakes up she looks out the window. Gray, storm-type clouds. The wind blows with a will of its own, like an old man wheezing. She realizes that autumn will soon swallow up summer's sparkling light.

THE ITALIAN IMMIGRANT'S MANUAL (1913)

On the habits of those residing in Argentina:

1. When a musical band plays the National Anthem, all present take off their hats as a sign of respect.

2. All women, whether ladies or washerwomen, are typically addressed as "señora." Calling a donna in town "mujer" does not sound nice, as this equates to female.

3. To call on someone at their home's front door, even when the door is open, do not bang or shout but clap your palms together three times.

4. To call a carriage or signal to a tram conductor from afar that he should stop, do not say "pss, pss, pss," which is not particularly sonorous, but "psciiiio, psciiiio."

5. In cafés or sweets shops there is always a special area reserved for señoras. The only men permitted are those accompanying them.

6. In a café or restaurant, call the waiter by clapping your palms twice and immediately saying "server!" which is what they say for waiter. Do not bang the table or your glass.

7. In theaters and cinemas, audience members are not permitted to wear hats, not even women, as this obstructs others from viewing the stage.

8. Do not smoke on trams or on the platform. The sign SPITTING PROHIBITED means vietato sputare.

9. To request the assistance of a police officer (watchman), who is also a civil guard (during emergencies such as fire, robbery, injury, violence, etc.), people use iron whistles, which many are in the habit of carrying in a pocket.

10. When out on the street, do not walk off the pavement: if you do, you will be called "atorrante" or tramp, which equates to beggar.

You're letting your imagination run wild, Gariglio said. Then added that kids are cruel, especially when it comes to their country. It's normal. But they're just words, get real, don't worry about it. We respect foreigners, he says. And Agustín feels reassured by the plural. As though by including himself in the sentence, his friend were signaling that he has the situation under control. And simultaneously excluding Agustín from that realm, casting him as an outsider. A safe outsider. They respected his mother, after all. No one had ever made Nélida feel like an intruder, despite her poor Spanish and chronic nostalgia. This town is full of Italians, the whole country is crawling with Italians. Right, so how could they not respect them. They came to this country to work the land, to increase the population, because that too was governing. To populate was to govern. Or was it the other way around? Either way, Agustín thinks, the Italians came to join ranks, not to fight us. The Chile thing, though, is a whole other story. People know little to nothing about the girl's country. They want a piece of our land, that's what people know. That if they had their way, they'd eradicate us from Patagonia. That their presidential palace was bombed, everyone knows that. And soldiers, sure, Agustín knows there are soldiers there too. Though he doesn't know if they have militias, if there is a people's army or something like it, the way there is here. We scare foreigners, but we'd never touch them, Gariglio insists. And lets out a laugh like a penknife stuck in his throat. But Chile is another story, Agustín insists. They want to take a piece of our land. Well, but that's not the girl's problem, Gariglio reasons. They're walking down Avenida Mitre at an easy pace. His friend is holding his bike on one side and they walk to the speed of its wheels. They smoke the three blocks between the typing academy and Agustín's house. Gariglio lives around the corner. Every Thursday the same. Sometimes they don't talk and one of the two will start whistling a song from the radio and then the other joins in, whistling backup. Agustín likes these interludes because he can let thoughts fly freely. Not like at home, where they get trapped between the walls and there comes a time when no one can get them out much less bring them back to life. Out on the street his thoughts take detours, don't stay inside the lines, soar into the sky and drift through space wherever they like. Agustín imagines Chilenita's house, back in her country. And him in it, suddenly in someone else's nest, on another's ground. He imagines himself accompanying her to visit her mother's grave, holding hands like two siblings who come from different geographical backgrounds but have inherited the same blood. Him like a big brother, as orphaned as she is but older. Almost a father. The pair of them carrying flowers, little piles of leaves and buds, to the grave of a mother who isn't Nélida. No, no parents, better with no parents from either here or there. With their own nest. Just the two of them, a couple of devils, in a land they themselves have besieged. Agustín and Ania burning the city down without anyone knowing who's behind the fire.

GREAT ENCYCLOPEDIA OF THE WORLD (1981), VOL. 24, PAGES 230-231:

Chile. Political evolution. *In the arena of international politics, in 1978, negotiations were entered into with Argentina over the old issue of the Beagle Channel, at the extreme southern tip of South America; these were broken once more, thereby necessitating the mediation of various countries as well as the Holy See.*

GREAT ENCYCLOPEDIA OF THE WORLD
(ERRATUM 1982), VOL. 24, PAGE 231:

Chile. Political evolution. *In the arena of international Politics, in 1978, negotiations were entered into with Argentina over border delineation in southern maritime areas, an issue which was finally brought before the Pope for mediation.*

Despite having fallen asleep effortlessly, Ania needs to be sure she's got enough sleeping pills. She doesn't know how many days she might end up staying in Campana. She has to listen for the phone, in case an interested party calls wanting to buy the properties. In case Claudia calls. It would appear that now she not only housesits but is a real estate broker as well. This makes her laugh, she feels ridiculously competent. She puts on the same clothes as the day before and leaves the house in search of a pharmacy. The air seems thicker this morning. On reaching Avenida Sarmiento, Ania gets the sense that the few inhabitants out and about are ignoring her. She looks herself up and then down till her chin hits her clavicle: she has to make sure it's her, that she's really there. For a second she actually thinks she's invisible. But no: Ania Coletti is in Campana. Ania Coletti has replaced her father and buried the last remaining member of the family. Ania Coletti has fulfilled her duty as planned and now has the feeling she's fled something she can't name. It seems inappropriate to awaken with words the images that have yet to arise.

Suddenly she's struck by the thought that she's forcing her way into some small, inland town, deep inside. Upriver on a new map. Without realizing it she whistles a tune. Any old tune, a cluttered sound that at one point may have been a song and come out of a transistor radio. She takes a side street and lets herself wander through the town's labyrinths. Attempting to follow her own rhythm, she walks down the footpath, not stepping on the cracks between paving stones. Closer to the river, the smoke grows thicker, increasingly solid. But Ania doesn't notice the burning smell, or the agonized song of cicadas charred in the nightly trash burning. Nor does she note the atmospheric changes that morning. Without warning, fat clouds cover the sky and then a few minutes later, like a mini-eclipse, the sun breaks through the thick smoke once more. Ania keeps whistling until, in one of the dark spells, she sees her own giant elongated shadow and is thrown. From one minute to the next she doesn't recognize herself in the slightest. It's as though she were her own double, taking a morning stroll through a set called Campana, by the branch of a river called Paraná. She can hear her breath, think her thoughts, observe herself from outside. From another galaxy. Her consciousness figures miles from her corporeal matter, so to speak, and suddenly she fears losing it forever. Ania has no clue where this new feeling might be coming from.

With the sense that she's about to disintegrate, she walks into a pharmacy that looks more like a department store and asks for her calmosedans, her zopiclones, her adormixes. The pharmacist gives her the look you'd give a Martian and assures her there's nothing like any of that around here. He's sorry, child. His tone is courteous but reserved. The tone of someone hiding something, of someone distrustful. And as she's on her way out of the pharmacy, the salesclerk stops her. How is Don Juan Coletti?, he asks. The man's words act like an intravenous drug. Ania doesn't even have time to wonder how this stranger could possibly know she's her father's daughter, Chilenita, the little Chilean. Instantly, she feels her bearing and carriage return, her spirit, her blood. Especially her blood. My father's doing well, she replies. Exceedingly well, she exaggerates her enthusiasm. Immediately she regrets this, but she's already left the pharmacy and is now walking toward the plaza.

On reaching the little bench beneath the jacaranda, next to the monument, she stops. The odd feeling from a few minutes ago has completely dissipated and she feels calm once more. Enough of this nonsense, Ania, she says to herself quietly. Take advantage of this, rest and relax now that you can. She gets up close to the monument and sees something she hadn't noticed the day before: above the immigrants' red letters, someone has spray-painted: "The only place for those who commit genocide is in jail." On the bench opposite, five or six old folks sit feeding pigeons and drinking maté. She glances sidelong at them and has the urge to approach and ask about the graffiti. Or, better yet, ask for a sip of maté and start playing a round of scopa with them. Sitting in the plaza in Campana, she laughs. The morning light is still flicking from sun to shadow, sun to shadow, like a lighthouse gone mad, but this no longer troubles her mind even infinitesimally. Ania breathes in deep and only then does she realize how heavy the air is. It smells like burning, she realizes, like burning leather.

My dear sister-inlaw: things have been done
haystily, I never thought Nélida should of
gone to america and now that she has you
can imagin how upset we are. i was thinking
maybe we woudnt see her again, if it was
up to me shed never have gone since its so
far and she had a good job close to home.
but her father insisted and whats done is
done. Shes never worked or done anyhting
around the house. given what happened she
was all ways afraid of getting to tired
which is why my daughter doesnt no how to
do anything domestick but youll teach her
your way. Treat Nelida like she's yours and
well know shes in good hands. we woud never
have sent her to america to be with you
other wise. Take her to Aroldo, their both
young and carefree.. if they have children
they'll keep them company and between one
thing and a nother they'll find there way.
It woudlnt make any sense to tell her whats
been done now, I know its not where she
really wants to be. We only hope god grants
her good health and it all goes well there
and time will tell. Love and blessings to
our dohter.
Send news soon,. Nina.

The setting for *Panic in Paradise* isn't real, Agustín thinks. Gariglio, on the other hand, argues that the place exists. That paradise exists. What exists is panic, Agustín says. You're just like your mother, always scared to death, the pair of you, Gariglio laughs. The storyline is predictable: a couple, on their honeymoon, travels to the place of their dreams. A small town on the coast, crimson sunsets, warm nights. Agustín thinks of Mar del Plata, the only beach he's ever been to. Though he's never seen a crimson sunset and hates warm air, whether at night or in the daytime. In any case, a few hours after their arrival, the novel's protagonists start to realize that something isn't right. The guests at the resort all walk slowly, drag their feet, their eyes half-closed. They take a few steps and vanish. They're like images in blurry photos, fading away. When the couple hears the others speak, they sound like robots: their voices send sparks flying from their mouths. The man and woman realize that life in this place has gone extinct and they are the only survivors. They realize, with increasing horror, that the creatures around them are specters of who they once were. And that they, she and he, are in transit, on their way to the other side. It's a matter of hours, of minutes. Gariglio says that what the book is trying to say is that paradise and hell are both figments of our imagination. That that's what makes them exist. What exists is panic, Augstín repeats. Gariglio bemoans the fact that his friend is such a birdbrain, that he always sees swamps where in fact there's dry land. Or maybe what he laments is that Agustín always interprets the stories so negatively.

When Ania gets back to the house she makes herself a cup of tea on the little stove and takes some water crackers out of her bag. She searches the pantry for sugar or some type of sweetener for her tea, and what she finds is something else. An enormous cardboard box. Where there should have been sugar, a box of Nélida and Agustín's belongings. That part she will learn in two minutes, when she opens it. Ania thinks, at that moment, that the box has been waiting for her since Nélida herself died and that it decided to appear before her now that Agustín has gone too. Now that she's buried him. As though together, from the afterlife, mother and son had made an agreement with the box and were sending Chilenita their belongings. They should have been in the house next door, but they're here. Okay, Ania, think. Don't go making up stories. The most logical explanation is that someone stored it over here on this side to keep it safe. But what for? She doesn't know. She looks for a knife in the kitchen but all she comes up with is a rusty fork. Burying it into the box, she watches the teeth bite into the cardboard. It's not easy, but she manages, chomping her way through with the fork. She gets the sense she's opening a window that's been sealed for too long. What she finds inside are photos sent from one continent to another, letters from Nélida's friends and relatives, passports, some type of guide for immigrants on how to behave, Agustín's baptismal certificate, workbooks, notebooks, a transistor radio and objects ranging from stamps to Italian lire.

Ania leaves her tea on one side, doesn't even touch the crackers. She doesn't know where to begin. The first thing she pulls out is a notebook covered in gift wrap, partially disintegrated from the damp and dust, with a sticker on the cover that reads: "Agustín Coletti. Typing." The handwriting is round, perfect. And then a date: March 1970. Agustín begins his notebook the exact year and month Ania is born. Agustín is writing random words, full of typos and sundry mistakes, as Ania is just beginning to babble. After that first notebook are fifteen or twenty more, spanning clear into the eighties. What they contain is exercises: words, sentences and various types of expressions, as though the student were tending the seeds of a language he'd never fully master, an alphabet of offcuts and errata, even though it's the language of his birth. As if his mother's and grandparents' Piedmontese had created some fissure, filling him with verbal insecurities, and he needed, urgently, to train his fingers, to connect them to a mind being invaded by fuzzy hairs. `Falkin`, `snell`, `howture`, `mermer`. Agustín has fallen into Nélida's things and now he's asking to be freed from the rubble. For a second, Ania thinks she should bring the notebooks to Javier and have him make a clean copy, restore them at the printer's. What Agustín types in the 1970 notebook are exercises: job application letters, collection notices, bills of sale. But also instructions on how to properly use a typewriter. And towards the end, words repeated across multiple lines, fifty, sixty times each. With countless typos. The cruel proximity of b to v on the keyboard might be a good excuse. But

Agustín's fingers or his lack of concentration or sloppiness go beyond that. The word "children" appears on several pages. Maybe it's easy to type, Ania thinks. The H with the right-hand index finger, next I with the middle, then L with the ring, all lined up. Nélida's child himself could have foregone the plural to make it even simpler. With four fingers he'd have fired off a steady stream of only children: child, bam-bam-bam-bam-BAM, child.

Of the various systems employed todate for the
instrecution of typing, the one that has proven
most efficient and offers them ost advantages
is unquesitonably the so-called Touch System,
as it is the only scientific on. In addition
to being the fastest its also the leaste tiring
to the typist, as the effort is distributed
evenly throughout the hand, thereby offering the
advantage of being able to type without so much
as glancing at the keyboard.

On the final page of Agustín's first notebook is a handwritten note, not in the same writing as what's on the cover but one that looks, to Ania, identical to her father's. She knows that that's impossible. The writing, surely, is Nélida's. Trying a different kind of writing, no longer rounded and perfect, so that her son will see that, like writing, life can be hostile too. "Grade: 5," it says. Ania isn't sure if this is on a 1 to 10 or 1 to 7 scale. In any case, it's not a good grade. She had to be stricter, more demanding, Ania's school inspector had told her. Had to keep tabs on the blunders the kiddies committed in their writing. Not hand out so many 7s, or the kids would get all fat and lazy. The inspector, so vigilant with her language, had said "get all fat." As if the students were piglets who needed to be fed controlled portions. This is what she thinks of now, so far from the children, a whole life away almost. She wonders then if the exercises of a boy typing furiously in an attempt to fill a mental void can be assessed with a grade, with empty numbers. She wonders if it really is Nélida grading him. And in that case, what she's grading, what she reads between the lines of these rambling phrases. Does mother realize that son is putting himself in her hands, in her fingers, to carry on the profession she abandoned, to follow, perhaps, her defective genealogy?

The phone rings but the stack of papers in Ania's hand clouds her hearing. Besides, it's very unlikely that the contraption would actually ring. It's impossible to process the bell as a genuine fact. Inside one of Agustín's notebooks she has found a batch of letters sent from Italy, addressed to his mother. She pictures Agustín discovering them at some point, after Nélida was already sick, and putting them away to keep them from getting ruined. The one she opens now is from Amelia di Pasquale. Date: December 12, 1973. "Te recordi quando eravamo contenti?" this Amelia person asks. And next she evokes, one by one, the greatest hits of their shared joy, lost between one continent and another. Country walks, swimming expeditions, Agustín. But this Agustín is not Aroldo's son, not her son. This is some prior character, someone Nélida had something with. Something that, to judge by her friend's letter, was both Nélida's infatuation and her undoing. The phone continues to ring. Now Giacomo, the father, writes. It's a letter several pages long, dated May 2, 1949, the day before Nélida set sail for America. A letter to be read aboard the ship, a farewell and a reassurance from afar, but also a manual. Be courteous but reserved with everyone, take great care around boys and don't trust them, be brave. She pictures Nélida on deck, very brave, reading the letter and glancing all around, ever alert for danger. She imagines her hurling herself into the ocean, slamming shut the escape route her parents had found her. The ship's sirens activated, a thousand emergency horns. Ania approaches the telephone, lifts the receiver and sets it back down. Courteous but reserved with everyone. The world is a very dangerous place, Ani. Her eyes close on their own, she leaves the material aside for a few hours. To breathe.

That night she takes one and a half zopiclones. She has ten left. Her sleep is thick, viscous. She sees Nélida and her family bidding her farewell at the seafront. She's wearing a hat with a veil that covers her face. Suddenly the image of Nélida's father turns into her own father. And Nélida is no longer Nélida but Leonora, covered by the same veil. It all blurs together now, she can't focus the scenes. Nor can she perceive any action or plot. When she wakes up, Ania tries to remember details of her dream, but someone else's handwriting has scribbled over the images and she finds nothing.

il pensiero di tuo   Torino 2-5-343   sta buona saluta tutti
papà ti seguirà sempre   Nelida cara dal momento
che ti trovi sola staccata da noi, ma sempre vicina,
ti accorgerai che ti manca qualche cosa, ma non
farci caso butta da parte nostalgia e malinconia
sorridi e guarda in faccia l'avvenire; che credo ti
sarà migliore del passato te lo auguro di tutto cuore

Ricorda e tieni sempre a mente i consigli e le
raccomandazioni che ti hanno sempre fatto i tuoi
genitori, primo fra tutti stare brava, cercare di farti
una compagnia buona se ti pare con le tue compagne
di cabina, cortese con tutti, ma riservata, non dare
confidenza ai giovanotti, perché sapendoti sola potrebbero
passare i limiti. Cerca di mangiare e bere e molto
riposo, non ballare, non preoccuparti anche se il
mare qualche giorno sia brutto, stai allegra e
vedrai che il tempo passerà più in fretta, guardati
dalle correnti di aria, tieni sempre la maglia di lana
sulla pelle anche se farà caldo, perché durerà solo pochi
giorni e avvicinandoti all'america farà più fresco.
Noi faremo sempre dire la preghiera che tu sai a
Lidia e ti nomineremo sempre così non ti dimenti
cherà tanto presto te diremo che sei dalla nonna
lontano lontano, anche tu qualche preghiera dovrai
ricordarti di dirla che sul vapore hai tempo da vendere,
buona fortuna e S. Rita ti aiuti ciao anche da Lidia

Quando sarai per o sai di partire ricorditi di far bene
e fai tutto li pericoli la vita bene e fai della tua
e fai tutto che conto che come di nuovo guardarti, vigore e ti obbligo
più che ti sia possibile così ti abbraccio tutti e tutte.

Guardati dai pericoli di cui è pieno il mondo special-
mente per voi ragazze, non dar retta, e ripeto confidenza
a nessuno, e non lasciarti o imbrogliare dalle chiacchiere
perchè i giovanotti non avendo niente da fare cercano di
passare il tempo. Se ti occorresse qualche cosa che non ti
sentissi bene non aver paura domanda che lì ci sarà il
medico ed hanno tutto quello che occorre. Fai attenzione
a tutto quello che ti porti, di non perdere niente sia la valigia
e quello che hai, quando arriverai a Buenos aires, non
aver fretta di discendere, preparate la roba e poi aspetti che
ti dicano di discendere, dirai che non sei pratica e che
aspetti che ti vengano a prendere, credo che se non ci
sarà subito i tuoi padrini, oppure Aroldo ricorda questo
nome, ti manderanno all'emigrazione e loro andranno
a prenderti la come ho fatto io. Quando scendi forse ti faranno
passare in un grande salone della dogana e ci saranno i
bauli tu cerca il tuo se sarai sola, e se c'è qualchediuno
te lo farai cercare così ti aiuteranno, credo che per una
ragazza anche i doganieri ti aiuteranno, dopo passata
la dogana chiudi bene il baule e lo legherai di nuovo
perchè dovrai poi spedirlo a Campana, ma spero che se
possono entrare ci sarà qualchediuno di loro ad aiutarti,
Tu tieni solo di vista il baule e valigia poi aspetterai anche
l'ultima a passare se non ci sarà ancora nessuno a
prenderti ma vedrai che andrà bene, e stai solo tranquilla
e calma ed allegra senza sempre.

Netità per aprire il baule prima tagli
la corda piccola col temperino, quella che
ha messo la dogana, poi sleghi quella
grossa adagio adagio senza tagliarla
così ti servirà ancora,

Fai bene attenzione a non perdere
niente ricordati di tutto, e se hai
bisogno di qualche cosa sul vapore
chiama non aver paura che ti
hanno tutto — A buenos aires
ricordati del ritratto di loro due e
poi se non è qualche uomo che non
ti sembra non andare finchè non
sii sicura se si presentasse per primo
Aroldo gli domandi come si chiama
anche in piemontese che lo capisce meglio
il suo cognome è Tortamagna.

Coraggio ed allegra che tutto andrà
bene, non aver paura del mare,
che ti farà ballare un po ma ti
divertirai e cercati una buona
compagnia sta brava come sai
che ti voglio dire tuo papà

L'indirizzo di tuo padrino

Francisco Damilano
Calle Moreno 325
(F.C.C.A.) Campana

AMENDMENTS AND CORRECTIONS: When a letter has been ommitted, and the error is not relaized until the end of the line,this is the way to proceed: Ifit is the last letter of a word, bring the carriage to the space between the incomplete word and the one following. If the missing letter is in the middle of a word, the entire incorrect word must be erase dand then retyped in the same space.

Ania knows the trains no longer run, but the following nights she hears a sound that can't be anything other than the huffing of a locomotive in the distance. The brakes or maybe some engine horn that scares off nocturnal birds and grows gigantic in its echo. If she concentrates hard, maybe it's not a train but a transverse flute. Dozens of flutes, pealing joyfully in the distance. Three nights running: the same sound in the wee hours. The sleeping pills don't even so much as tickle her. Lack of sleep is making her irritable, grumpy. She ought to go out, buy supplies, get some air. Ania thinks it makes no sense to be here, she should go back to Chile and finally face up to things. What things? Her existence, what else. But she realizes that this thought is not entirely her own. There's something moving around in there without her will, in her head, something she can't fully grasp. The fourth night, she gets up, uncovers the typewriter and begins to type the first thing that appears: sentences run wild, images banged out like drums. She needs to deaden the sound of the train that isn't a train. It strikes her that she should hear some different voices. Go buy batteries for Agustín's radio and listen to any old station, whichever one the world sends her right now. Walk into town and demand greetings from whoever she runs into, require some cordiality of them, walk into Cecil's, talk to the barkeep, find the señoras' section, order a very cold beer, walk out with the bottle in her hand and find the cybercafé Gariglio told her about at the funeral, send Javier an email. How's the cat? Is he getting used to things, has he forgotten me? Or better yet, call her father: How's Leonora's convalescence coming along? The kids, grandkids, rat dog? Yes, Agustín is underground now, yes, you can rest easy. I'm here. I'm you. Send me some little cans of shellfish. Forget it, it was a joke. You should be here with me, papi. Right this moment she'd like to go outside and smoke, but she hasn't lit up a cigarette in forever, not since when she was at university. She suspects she no longer knows how to smoke. Ania would like to blow smoke out her mouth on some train platform, step off the pavement, wear a straw hat in the theater, bang her glass on the table to call the waiter at Cecil's, be a lady or a washerwoman, a female, call a tram with some very marked pss-pss-pssing. She'd like to add a few points to Nélida's manual. Counterpoints: do not compete with either the dog or your father's wife, do not try to find yourself in photos on others' walls, do not live through others' lives, do not expect the dead where no one has summoned them, have a garden and water it by night, do not see mountains as geographical accidents but as biographical branches, cry at others' funerals as well as your own, especially your own, climb into attics as if climbing a mountain. That's what she needs to do: dare to climb the stairs to the attic and bring her memory face to face with the ruins.

BACKSPACE: This is normally situate don the upper right hand-side although on some machines it maybe found on the left. It works the opposite of the others; striking this key; the carriage backs up one space.

She straightens the bed covers, pulls open the curtains and throws on the first clothes she finds at hand: the same faded jeans she traveled in, the same sweatshirt as the funeral. This time she leaves the lettering on display: *Are you ready?* What might she be ready for? Ania wants to look at herself in the mirror but realizes that there isn't a single one in the whole of her grandparents' house. Not in the bathroom not in the hallway certainly not in the bedrooms. She looks to see her reflection in the window: a thin silhouette, almost without form. A few lopsided locks, bowerbird-like, or like some kind of bird anyway. At least she exists—relief. She approaches, determined, the attic stairs. She walks up as cautiously as she would if crossing a hanging bridge suspended over the ocean. The stairs creak, at any minute the whole structure will come tumbling down and she'll be there, alone, unconscious, and no one will know. Ania thinks she's being seized by the spirit of Gariglio's horror stories. Or worse, by the bellicose spirit of the days when Nélida had yet to set sail for this side of the world. She tries to return to her own era, to laugh at these notions, but the sound that comes out more resembles a sneeze than a giggle. She reaches the top step, thinking that everything is under control, but on opening the attic door, unexpected memories slip in without anyone having summoned them. Her at Claudia's school, her cousin's look of shock or fear, mouth open and eyes fixed on a point just behind Ania's head that Ania cannot see, and immediately afterward, the blow to the back of her skull and the silence and the shadow of a boy or a fleet-footed midget running off with a stick in his hand and then unconsciousness and then a much denser silence, and opening her eyes and the expressions on the faces of onlookers peering through the car window, the dogs barking in the distance, the car seat stained with her blood, a thick viscous substance, and whose car was she deposited in, with her head bleeding and her hair matted in scarlet liquid, and why were they taking so long to leave for the hospital, the same hospital where Nélida went in and then came out another, a woman who'd lost her head, a hollowed out body, the same hospital where Agustín stopped being a body and became a remain: all of that now seeps into her scrambled thoughts, as she enters the attic and finds that the bedspread is the same, the cobwebs make it nearly impossible to see the window and the ceiling fan blades are all broken, as are the plates, the orange tree's branches, the certainties of adolescence, the mirrors in this house, the little butterfly legs on the road. All of this suddenly appears and, even if she closes her eyes and opens them back up again, she can't make it go away. Then she walks back down the staircase and feels, step by step, that she is once more becoming the person she was when she saw the light this morning.

TOUCH POSITION: Students must get used to sitting in a confortable, upright position, leaning against back of the chair. They must be niether to close nor to far from the typewriter. Arms should be almost parallel, hanging naturally from the body, and must remain relaxed but motionless and loose. Hands should be together over the keyboard, the pinky fingers of the right and left hand, when not reeaching to strike other letters, resting gently over the A and the Ñ respectively, so that the index fingers can reach the letters G and H with relative ease. The thumbs will be almost touching, resting over the space bar.

The sound of the bell rouses her. It's not the phone, this time somebody is there in person, flesh and blood, somebody who knows she's inside. She has no idea what time it is, could be morning or afternoon. She's lost all sense of time, and the light filtering in through the window has no character. It's a flat light, lacking in sparkle or gradation. The sound she hears now is not that of transverse flutes. It's a bell, at the door, that much is clear. Who could be ringing the doorbell of an uninhabited, ramshackle house, one that shows no signs of any living presence? Let them dingdong away, let the invader's finger get stuck there. She thinks she ought to blow an iron whistle and ask a police officer for help, but that would be overkill. There's no danger in a doorbell, Ania, take it easy. Then she stops worrying about it and returns to the typewriter. She leans back against the chair, searching for a comfortable upright position. Arms loose and relaxed. Hands together over the keyboard. She goes over the notes she sketched out the night before. Thinks that from now on she should record each of her steps. Those of the present but also those that came earlier. Go back and then zigzag her way up to today. Leave a trace. But who for? And more importantly, what for? After thinking about this for a minute, she exhausts her options and her options exhaust her. She'd have to put herself in other people's shoes, not just their houses. Not simply look after their property: merge with them, become them. That's what she'd have to do. Learn from Nélida, from her great-grandparents, who were able to release their origins and became others. She can't entrust herself to her own miniscule story. Besides, she makes too many typos, her fingers don't fly at the speed Nélida's no doubt did. Her clumsiness is akin to Agustín's and yet hers has other origins. She's used to the tiny buttons on her cell phone, even if she does hate using it. The typewriter keys are stiff, they resist. She thinks she should write her father. Counsel him to be brave and take great care, warn him that it's rude not to include your daughter in family photos, not to bury your cousin, to switch sides; tell him not to spit in the street, that only tramps do that. Her father needs to straighten up, and she can guide his behavior from his birthplace. From the dining room, sitting at Nélida's typewriter, which became Agustín's typewriter, she regards her father's room. She can't picture him here, it's so hard to envision. The night before, she took the pictures down off the wall. Nélida's and the rest of the family's. She lay them face down, next to the photo of the boy who would become her father. If she can't see herself in the mirror, they can't either. Disappear once and for all, altogether. Arranged like that, upside down on the table, the pictures look like playing cards from a game left unfinished. The bell rings again. Ania leaves the typewriter on one side and heads to the door. She's not sure what she'll do when the intruder is right there in front of her. She should be prepared, have a weapon for self-defense, but it's too late. No way to stop her steps now. It seems such a long way, she feels like someone is stretching the floor, making it infinite. Like it was exercise equipment or one of those moving floor things at the airport intended to accelerate passengers' progress. She thinks she's not going to make it to the door, that she'll never leave this spot on the map. That the house will fall down with her inside it, devoured by time.

The town in *The Evil Inheritance* has been beset by an epidemic of insomnia. The infection is spread through breathing. After going three hundred twenty days without sleep, the infected die. The horrible thing is that their eyes remain open for all eternity. The town is soon inhabited by zombie-people, stupefied with sleep. Time is all out of whack. A pill that cures the disease is discovered, but it costs a fortune. The few who can get their hands on it turn miserly and hoard all the doses. But soon, something happens. Those who have taken the pill, after sleeping marvelously for thirty nights in a row, stop waking up. The narrator of the story is an infected woman who's gone three hundred nineteen nights without sleep. She doesn't have much time left. Her children, her husband, her nieces and nephews, her friends: they've all succumbed. They never had access to the pill, so their deaths were long and tortuous. The woman lives surrounded by corpses, because the gravediggers can't work fast enough to bury all the bodies littering the streets. She goes out afternoons, rifles through clothing of the dead, plundering their bodies, no longer knowing what for. All those sleepless nights likely caused her to lose her mind. At any rate, one afternoon she finds one of the pills in a dead man's pocket. A man who, in his mortuary aura, has beautiful, pearl-colored eyes. What to do? The woman debates: take the pill so as to die in her sleep thirty days later or ignore it and die of sleep in a few hours, eyes open. Then she lies down on the sidewalk, beside the pearly-eyed corpse, and waits for the sun to set.

Ania doesn't understand how it is that this man is here before her. She's lying on the floor and he's stroking her head. She sees a pimply face, a face that has perpetuated the marks of adolescence until well into its seventies. A man with an ancient brown beret. For a minute she thinks it's Agustín. But as soon as she really opens her eyes, she sees the man's mouth open. And hears: it's me, Gariglio. Are you okay? There's something in his expression, she's not exactly sure what, something indecipherable that Ania now connects with Javier. Maybe it's the way his eyes look sort of slanted, as if someone were behind him, pulling back the skin and not letting go. Maybe it's the large, slightly calloused hands. How she wishes it were Javier there before her. Javier and, behind him, the cat. Either of the cats: his or hers, the gray or the orange. An animal, and the calm that comes of being on solid ground. I guess I fell but I'm fine, she says, to say something. The man stops stroking her head and she makes sure there's no blood. None visible, anyway. She's not sure if she managed to open the door and then collapsed or Gariglio forced his way in or what. Thank you, thank you, thank you, she repeats while attempting to rouse herself. Stop saying thank you, the man says. And then he offers her a maté. He offers it to her, not her to him. Then he pushes back his beret in a relaxed, domestic gesture, as if he were the homeowner. Ania gets her head together. She stands slowly but steadily, goes to the kitchen, puts water on the stove and offers the visitor a seat. Do you really remember me?,

Gariglio asks with a childlike expression. Ania comes clean: I remember you as Agustín's shadow. Skinny Gariglio looks away, sees the typewriter, the stacks of paper piled on either side, the letters, typing notebooks, battery-operated radio, all of Ania's father's cousin's belongings. Now he rests his gaze on a picture ID-sized photo of Agustín. An image that reminds Ania of Elvis. Gariglio's eyes tighten, his blinking seems to accelerate. Impossible to know what thoughts are crossing his mind at this precise moment. "They're all gone," the man whispers. Ania isn't sure whether his words are addressed to her or not. Just in case, she doesn't reply. Where once there'd been a pencil, now Gariglio stashes a cigarette. Suddenly he seems to recall that it's there. He takes it out, prepares to smoke. He doesn't ask permission and she doesn't grant it. It is a fact. She brings matches and the maté from the kitchen and settles beside him, at the table with the typewriter and the found objects. Neither of them speaks for a spell, they let the embers burn the paper and tobacco in the cigarette, making an almost inaudible sound, the same noise a spider would make weaving its web or they themselves letting air in and out of their lungs. Until Ania breaks the silence and asks where the internet place is. The Uruguayans' place, the one Gariglio mentioned at the wake. She lost the scrap of paper, she says. She wants to write her people, she says. Only then does the man seem to disengage from his thoughts and respond that that's precisely why he came, to see if she needed any help. You sure you're okay, dove? Truly, I'm absolutely fine. Ania is about to ask him precisely the same thing, and then doesn't. They share two or three matés and leave the house, heading for the center of town.

Three days left till Chilenita's father comes. Every night it's the same: the locomotive wakes him to sound the alarm. Just get your things and do it, Tinito. It's your turn now. Agustín covers his ears with the pillow but the noise is still there, like a blind arrow stuck in his skull. What he should do is get up noiselessly, find a coat, grab a few tins from the pantry, a bunch of cigarettes, a couple novels and Nélida's cards so he won't get bored on the road. Put the typewriter in one of the yeast bags, pack it all into his mother's suitcase and go out through the back door without anyone hearing him. Bring a hand to his heart as a farewell to his parents. On the shared patio, cut down a couple bunches of grapes for the road. Silently open the door to the other house and sneak in like a bandit, walk stealthily, not turning on a single light, go by touch. Climb up the stairs, to the attic. Approach Chilenita. Tell her to keep quiet, please, to help him. Cover her mouth if she puts up a struggle. Tell her to help him out, not be afraid. It would be terrible to scare her grandparents at this time of night. If the girl accepts willingly, on the other hand, take her hand and retrace his steps with her, two prisoners on the lam. Go down the stairs, through the hall, open the door and out onto the street. Consider stopping at Gariglio's to say goodbye. Discard the idea. Run to the train station. Listen to the sound of the transverse flutes welcoming them like a couple of siblings accursed by some ancient misfortune. Take the first train. Give Chilenita a little slap to calm her down, if she struggles. Or light a cigarette and start to plan their days in an alien land. Think: good God, we're going to be so happy! Smoke on the platform and the train, forget about whether or not it's permitted. Teach the girl to blow smoke out through her nose, teach her to type with all ten fingers, get her out of her bubble. Establish a new code of conduct for this familial stampede. On reaching Villa Ballester set the typewriter on the little table between their two seats, and give her a dictation. Number one: forget about your previous life. Number two: do not latch on to any one place. Number three: do not listen to strangers' nonsense. Number four: do not build a nest on foreign soil. Number five . . . Why isn't the girl obeying? Why has she stopped typing and now begun running down the corridor and hurling herself from the train and climbing onto a locomotive headed the other way and sticking her head out the window and showing him the book in her hand, *The Evil Inheritance*, and waving goodbye and she's not alone, the girl, but with her father and they're going back to Chile, together, like the couple of foreigners they will always be and leaving him alone in the prison that Agustín can't stand? Every night that infernal whistle. Sometimes he thinks he's going to lose his mind, like his mother herself did. Better to make a little space for yourself in the back seat of the Citroën and refuse to get out for anything in the world. Root yourself to that spot, man. Nail yourself down. Become one of those butterflies the girl likes to save. Present her with your legs and your antennae, and let her wipe the dust off your wings with her savior's fingers.

THE ITALIAN IMMIGRANT'S MANUAL (1913)

Truffa all'americana, the "story of my uncle" or double-crossing

Now that I've taught you to move about the city, and before pointing out the famous and beautiful things, I am once more going to remind you of the recommendations I was obliged to make regarding the city from which you set sail: "On guard against swindlers." There I told you they abound, here I will say they are legion. Distrust anyone without the proper attire or authority to approach, pay no heed to tales of wonder or sob stories and remain, for the time being, steadfastly unable to lend the slightest hand to anyone, particularly anyone who claims to have "made the journey with you," which one never knows whether or not to be true. Beware of the renowned system used to deceive immigrants who have just disembarked: the so-called "story of my uncle," flimflam that in Italy is known as the *truffa all'americana*.

Somebody stole Gariglio's bike. The day after Agustín's funeral, right at his own front door. Nothing like that had ever happened: for years he had the same bike and parked it in the same place, at the same time. This city's not like it used to be, he says, getting to be there's nobody left you can trust. Actually, getting to be there's nobody left at all, he adds quietly. They are walking down Belgrano, slowly, like a couple of old folks who've lost their way and their urgency. Ania has the impression that all the city's streets look the same except for the avenues. Sarmiento, Mitre, and La Rocca are rivers with moderate flow. The rest— Paso, Colón, Arenales, Jautes, all the streets around her grandparents' house, including Calle 9 de Julio itself—are just streams, creeks down which the residents move to get from the ice cream parlor to the pharmacy, from the market to Cecil's, from the hospital back home. As if picking up the thread of an interrupted conversation, Gariglio now asks about her findings. He wants to know if, in among the heap of papers and photos, she found any letters Agustín kept. Letters? No, Ania says. Just notes from typing class, his notebooks. Should there have been letters?, she asks. No idea, Gariglio replies. But it's not a convincing response. It's an expression that translates to a shrug of shoulders: how would I know? There's an ugly silence, which lasts two or three minutes. One of those silences so awkward they're loud. Then Gariglio interrupts it by whistling for two blocks straight. A catchy tune, a little Peruvian waltz, Ania thinks. His whistle carries them to the safety of the internet place. And there are the Uruguayans, made aware of her presence in advance, anxious, it would appear, to receive her and offer her their ancient wireless contraption. So you're Coletti's daughter?, says one of the two, the man or the woman. Ania has the sense that they said it in unison. This is Chilenita, Gariglio corroborates. Ania, she says, my name is Ania. But they Uruguayans pay no attention. Or else her voice had no volume. Skinny Gariglio now tells them that she, Chilenita, is staying at the house on Calle 9 de Julio. Her grandparents' house, not Agustín's. She's going to be here for some time, he says. Ania doesn't contradict him. She sits in front of the only computer there is, an enormous monitor, turbines going full throttle, and hears the conversation they continue having as a distant murmur. She catches random words: "funeral," "family," "Chile." She feels like they're scanning through her life behind her, and she can't do anything about it, she's fallen into a trap. The connection takes its time going through, but after a while she manages to get into her email. Finally the screen offers her silence, and once connected she can disconnect from the conversation behind her back. She has messages from the owner of a dog she walks and someone who needs her to water their plants the following week. There are bank notices too, and other irrelevant messages she doesn't even open. But not a thing from Javier or her father. Six days and not a word, as if the mountains and the pampas had cut the cord that tied them. A silence she doesn't dare interpret. She writes to Javier:

she's fine, she has to wait for the house stuff to go through, things have happened, please send signs of life. She writes to her father: she's fine, she has to wait for the house stuff to go through, things have happened, can he send money so she can extend her stay in Campana. Please. She stays online for a bit, to see if a reply from one of the two comes in. She goes to a page with international news. Headlines that mean nothing to her. "Egypt sentences poet to three years for song against Al Assisi." Next page: "Valuable 17th-century Swedish crown jewels stolen." Next: "Wrens becoming baritones." She clicks on the article. Certain urban-dwelling birds, like the wren, are developing more complex calls so that their natural songs are not drowned out by city sounds, the story explains. The calls, which the birds use for both courtship and warning, have become deeper and longer in order to be heard. They've learned to become others, Ania thinks. That's what I ought to do when I go back: change my voice, lower the tone a notch, make my call more complex. Gariglio glances at her from the corner, as though seeking approval for something he just said. She plays along and says yes, yes, yes. The Uruguayans laugh. Their laughter seems to come through a very narrow tunnel. Ania gazes at the screen and manages to cloud her eyes. She clouds her ears too. She's unsure how many minutes she remains like that, frozen in time and space. At some point Gariglio touches her shoulder and asks if she's okay. Absolutely fine, she replies. She looks at her email again: nothing. No new messages. Ania goes to take a few bills from her pocket to pay, but the Uruguayans say don't even think about it, it's on the house, a courtesy. Were you able to contact your people?, Gariglio asks as they retrace their steps. Yes, she says simply. She suspects the man would like to know more but doesn't give him that pleasure.

When they're almost to Calle 9 de Julio, Ania asks about the horror novels. Do you still have them? Gariglio says he gave the whole lot to Agustín years and years ago. They must be in the house next door, the one Ania hasn't gone into yet. Do you need them?, the man asks. Ania says no, she was just curious. I could go in with you if you feel a little scaredy, Gariglio says. Why would he think she's scared? Why does he make it diminutive? Why is he treating her like a dipshit? The questions pile up, one after the other, but don't leave her mouth. Instead she says she's fine, thank you, that she doesn't feel scared, not even a little scaredy.

GREAT ENCYCLOPEDIA OF THE WORLD (1981),
VOL. 24, PAGE 144:

Calculator (pocket). *The spectacular advances in applied electronics made in the mid-sixties, in particular the development of MOS circuits and ROM memory, gave rise, with the emergence of pocket calculators during the seventies, to an expansion as great as that seen in the branch of radio receivers after the invention of the transistor.*

In last night's dream, Agustín is with Elvis Presley. The musician is giving a concert in a bar that, in the dream world, Agustín frequents regularly. He knows the place like the back of his hand, is pretty sure he could find his way around blindfolded. In the middle of the bar is a makeshift stage with a red curtain backdrop. At the table with Agustín are Gariglio, Chilenita's father, and others. But he, Agustín, is the one Elvis is looking at. He is the one he sings to, the one he winks at mischievously. And then he invites him up onstage. His companions applaud, whistle, go bananas at the invitation Elvis extends. Chilenita's father urges him on. Go, don't be silly, he says. Don't be daft, Gariglio chimes in. But he doesn't dare. Suddenly he's forgotten all the words to the songs, his mind has gone blank. He wishes Nélida were there so she could help him remember the words, so they could sing together for the Campana crowd and he could find the voice and elegance of his idol. You look like an angel, walk like an angel, talk like an angel. But I got wise. You're the devil in disguise. Oh yes, you are. You're the devil in disguise. Elvis climbs down off the stage to get him and when he's right there, about to take his hand, Agustín realizes it's not Elvis Presley but Skinny Gariglio who is taking his hand to pull him up onstage. He can't

122

see if the other Gariglio, the one who was with him at the table until that moment, has split into two, or disappeared. He also doesn't get to find out what happens onstage after that, whether he climbs up or not, whether he sings with the phony Elvis or not. He wakes up right before the end.

Agustín, esta
es tu mamá con el
pelo corto y la
guitarra. escuché
ya muchos discos
de Elvis Presley.

Ania doesn't sleep that night. The two zopiclones pass right on through, her body doesn't even register them. No sooner does day begin to dawn than she gets out of bed. Obeying the command of some internal order, something that's not logic yet nor is it brute sentiment. Something that came before her, she thinks, is forcing her to act. The mornings have started to get cold. The warmest thing she has in her suitcase is the black sweatshirt. At this rate she doesn't care if the lettering is facing in or out. No sweatshirt is going to tell her whether she's ready or not. She has the sense the cicadas are singing at a higher pitch than on previous days, just the opposite of the wrens, she thinks. She presumes they finally adapted to the loud laughter of the old folks in the plaza. Ania decides that she's going over to the other side, to Nélida and Agustín's place. This is it. They're all gone and she needs to see the space before it is demolished or refurbished. She feels she's just flapping around in circles and needs to trounce her inertia. Ania doesn't know what's behind that door. Darkness, what else? Toward the end of her days, when Nélida was hardly even Nélida anymore and Ania would visit, the woman would ask her not to turn on the lights. She didn't want to see them, she'd say. If any light came in, they'd take her with them, she would insist, lowering her voice. And she'd squeeze the hand or the leg or whatever foreign body part was closest to her tightly, as though the flesh itself could keep her this side of existence. Ania didn't dare ask who *they* were, who would take her away. Nélida would be silent, return for a few minutes to a precarious kind of calm. And then after a while she'd bring her hands to her head and move her fingers slowly, in a very meticulous to and fro. Ania imagined the woman was plucking out her thoughts with a tweezers, one by one, like splinters. And arranging them in an imaginary little row for the wind to scatter. That way they'd dissolve, Ania thought, the bad stuff would vanish. It struck her at the time that Nélida's mind was the one that dreamed up the horror stories that Agustín lent her, Gariglio's novels, the same novels that must now be all moth-eaten or mouse-eaten inside there. But the demons in those stories never truly took hold in Ania's head. They were too simple to take seriously. Nélida's, on the other hand, were always more dangerous. Because they were closer and stayed in the family. She wanted to know if her great-aunt's dead were also her dead. So she listened to her, equally possessed by those ungovernable apparitions. Now she realizes that Agustín and Nélida lived under the sway of the same darkness, which was not the darkness of death but that of unruly, possessed thoughts, like tornadoes lashing the pampas.

She doesn't quite know how, but she made it across the shared patio and is now at the door. She knows she must act, that she must finally enter the kingdom of ghosts and critters governing this cavern once and for all. That this will be the last thing she does in Campana, she already knows. Push the door open, cross the border. It takes some doing, but after several tugs, the wood yields. Gloom, spiderwebs, a stale smell. It's what she imagined, all in all. In Agustín's room she finds an unmade bed, a ton of medication, dirty clothes strewn on the floor, dozens of cigarette butts in three or four ashtrays and the remains of several mosquito coils. No leftovers, no animal corpses of any kind, no posthumous message, no treasures to unbury. She supposes Agustín spent his days in the other house and only slept and smoked over here. Nélida's room, on the other hand, is empty. With the exception of that green wooden floor that, just like the typewriter and other belongings, had been waiting for her, unflappable, all these years. Ania recognizes it immediately: being seated there, listening to the raspy, exhausted voice coming from her great-aunt's throat. They were so young, she was so young, the soldier Agustín. Then she contradicts herself. A friend. Her Gs like Cs: a cood friend, she says, from the neighborhood. He was an old classmate from secondary school, he was her teacher, they worked together at the factory. She used to smoke in the plaza or on the river bank with this Agustín, far before her son Agustín. Sometimes they'd go to the movies, he in his just-pressed uniform and his olive-green cap. The pounding of bombs, the country invaded, she says. The sirens. Armed men and tanks on every corner, the fires, the houses ransacked, the family fleeing through the countryside. One time she bought him cigarettes. Correction: one time she was walking down the street in town with a bag full of cigarettes for a relative. Contraband cigarettes. And the soldiers detained her and took the cartons and other things. Right in the middle of the plaza, in plain sight, with everybody there acting like they were blind. The pounding of the whole province, and the blow to the head and then unconsciousness and a dense silence. Cigarettes strewn all over the ground. Her whole body, Agustín, her clothes, all the cigarettes. There were dogs all around, hungry beasts. She didn't inhale the smoke, she didn't know how to blow smoke out through her nose, she choked. Another version: one time the soldier offered her cigarettes and she turned him down and kept walking, swaying her hips left to right, right to left, in a little imaginary military march. Over there, the war; her here. Agustín, again Agustín. Barking, correction, screaming. Nélida gets mixed up when she tries to recount the scenes to Chilenita. That's all, Ania realizes: a lone green floor, attesting to the memory of a house in ruins. No sign of the horror novels. That's all, she concludes. And she sits on the green floor to await something she knows will not happen.

KEYSTROKES: For proper typing it is
essential that one observe certain rules:

1: Keys must be tapped gently and sharply,
lifting ones fingers as quickly as
possible.

2: The force of each tap should be the
same for all letters. In thi sway, the
text will be even througuoht,.

3 The speed should be uniform,
endoveroing, to the degree possible, to
type rithmically, that is, leaivng the
same amount of time by tween each stroke.

Two days till Chilenita's father comes. The rumors he heard are spreading. Agustín knows the kids lower their voices when he passes. "One of the fucking Chilean's family," he hears them whisper now, on the opposite side of the street. Still, to the boys at school, their being family lends him a tiny glimmer of light, removes his anonymity. At least he exists. The idea of breaking his silence once and for all, joining their anonymous voice crosses his mind. Leave his cave, put himself on the other side of danger, cross that ocean. Here I am, what do you want?, he's about to say. But that's not him. Agustín wants to run to Chilenita's rescue. Nélida would be grateful, he's sure of it. Gariglio told him that kids are cruel, that heaven and hell exist. He doesn't know what to think. They're just kids, they can't do much harm, he tries to convince himself. They're the same age as his mother's nephew, the one that died in her arms. Younger than Chilenita, than her cousin Claudia. They're nonentities, he tries to think. But he also knows that rage runs thick, that the motherland is not a question of age. He's got less than forty-eight hours to do something. He can't fail her the way he failed his mother. Can't let history repeat itself. He's got it: join the boys and keep the girl from leaving. No, no, no, not that. Hold her captive, not let her go. Hide her from everyone, even her father. Everyone knows parents take root in their children's bodies and have to be driven out by force. Or, even better, much better, how did he not think of this before: kidnap the girl and hand her in at a detention center. Take her there wrapped in an Argentine flag. Tell them Chilenita's father is a leftie, say it the way he's heard other people say it: that shitbag is a leftie, ran away to Chile the way shitbag lefties always do. Say it just like that. Add that they can use the girl as a hostage. And offer to guard her. That way he could spend all day with her, teach her, get her straightened out, start from scratch. What are you saying, my God, Tinito. What you have to do is obvious. So he crosses the street and walks over to the boys. Right, what's the problem? I'm Chilenita's uncle, he says.

From the darkness of Nélida's room she hears the phone ringing in the other house. The little bell tinkling like a fire alarm brings her back to reality. She lets it express itself for a spell, till the sound fades away. After ensuring that, cicadas aside, silence has once more prevailed, she abandons her position on the little green floor and goes to the empty space previously occupied by Nélida's bed. It looks to her like the house is a deserted hospital and the ill, the trivial, and the terminal have gone forever. Only then does she prepare to leave. She considers her options: take a siesta under the revolving blades of the ceiling fan, like she used to do with her grandparents, or head to the internet café and check her email again. She opts for the latter. She needs some fresh air inside her head. Ania grabs her bag and locks the front door, in case it takes her a while to get back. She decides to eschew the most direct route to town so as not to bump into Gariglio. She walks several blocks towards the center, bypassing the main streets, till she gets to Cecil's. Peering through the large front window, she sees the dimly lit interior. Behind the counter, a gray-haired man, on realizing he is being watched, smiles timidly. Ania wonders if he recognizes her. If this man, too, knows she's Coletti's daughter. Lateral light illuminates the strain of a fake smile, and now the man's whole figure is reflected in the window. She moves her gaze from the café's interior to its entrance. A bicycle that looks very much like, or the same as, Gariglio's is chained to a post by the door. For a second she's afraid the man will appear like a ghost at the café's bar and ask her to have a drink with him. She looks around, tries to get her bearings. She's lost her sense of direction and no longer knows where the internet place is. The expected ensues: Gariglio sticks his nose out the door and gives her a quiet shout. What are you doing here, dove? Are you lost? And yes, she is lost. And no, she doesn't want a drink. And thank you, oh, thank you so much. Though she says it's not necessary, Skinny Gariglio escorts her to the internet café and then goes back to Cecil's. The Uruguayans recognize her immediately. Chilenita can't go a day without connecting to the world, eh?, they joke. Ania doesn't find it amusing, but doesn't say anything. She sits in the same chair as the day before and switches on the monitor. The thing takes several minutes to connect. And when it does: disappointment. No sign of her father or Javier. For a second she thinks she no longer exists. The dead don't receive email, Ania, get with it. Then she realizes: there are more than thirty unread messages in her junk folder. And that's where Javier's are, dancing on the screen. The first is seven days old. "Important," reads the subject line. It irks her that Javier is so literal. If something is important, you don't announce it, you just spit it out, she thinks. And makes a mental note for her manual of conduct. For a few seconds she avoids opening it. She doesn't want to learn about something deemed "important" with such fanfare. Words are ammunition, Javier should know that. She thinks she should have taken that siesta at her grandparents' house instead of coming to the cybercafé. She thinks about the importance of being someone else, of being suspended in time. But that's not it, that's really not it. What the subject line in fact triggers is panic. Why is Javier preparing her with this warning? What is to follow that's so important? And then she knows, and opens it. "Your father hospitalized," Javier has written. Like it was a telegram, as short as possible. Like it was the seventies and he was economizing on words. Three words sent, zero expense. Three sharp taps, projectiles straight to the heart. How hard would it have been to add a verb: is, was, will be. Your father *was* hospitalized, but he's out now. Don't worry, girl. Your father *will be* hospitalized if you don't return. React, woman. Your father *is* hospitalized and there's nothing that can be done. Sorry, daughter. Her touch system fully deployed, Ania takes a deep breath and prepares to open Javier's other messages.

THE ITALIAN IMMIGRANT'S MANUAL (1913)

Punishment aboard the ship. Discipline can be imposed
on anyone who violates regulations, disturbs the order,
commits a moral offense, wrecks things or does not
respect others' rights. One can also, if so deserved, be
put in jail and spend the night on the ship's bridge with
the helmsman.

They cracked the girl's head open. That afternoon, around two, she went to meet her cousin at school and the boys detected enemy presence. "Chile, go home!" they shouted. And the stick to the back of skull—"Take that, intruder!"—and the blood and the boys running off. Agustín heard it from Gariglio. It made him want to grab the same stick and break it across his friend's ribs. For not believing him, for treating him like a worrywart. There's my wild imagination, right there. Now he might lose her forever: Chilenita won't want to come back to Campana anymore, she won't. Agustín knows that some years ago, the girl's father got his head cracked open too. Not because he was Chilean, which he wasn't, but because . . . he's not really sure why. The thing with her father didn't happen at a school but at university, over in the capital, on the orders of the new government. That was years ago, nobody even remembers it anymore. Agustín was told that his cousin had gotten his head sewn up, seven stitches he got, and the second he recovered he took off to Chile forever. And that's where the girl was born, Chilenita, who is now getting eight more stitches, Agustín learns. A clean sweep if you're playing scopa: seven plus eight, fifteen. Perfect hand. Chilenita and her father with their heads drawn on, fifteen stitches like the dotted

lines on tourist maps. Like the one they use when going to
Mar del Plata, to Mendoza, to Chile too. Her father will take
her away tomorrow or the day after, as soon as the girl is
better. There's nothing Agustín can do. He plans to visit her
in the hospital and walk down the same corridors he walked
down when his mother took the bottle of pills. That time he
couldn't save her. At least with Chilenita he tried. He tried
to stop the ambush, and instead all he did was fan the flames.
A fucking booby, that's what he was. The boys had laughed
in his face. Said if he was the Chilean's uncle, he'd get what
he deserved too. He was a traitor, they said, the family of an
enemy is the enemy too. Get out of here, scram, they said.
Shouted. Get out of here, dumbass, go! And he told them
to go fuck themselves, but said it very quietly. Silently, to
himself, actually, not out loud. What he did, in fact, was take
off. Exactly as the boys ordered.

The Uruguayans say that it's taken care of, that there's no charge for the service, that they're very sorry, sweetheart. Seven minutes is how long the call to Santiago lasted. Seven days is how long the messages were there without her seeing them. Without realizing what was really important, without knowing how to interpret the silence. Seven days of not answering the contraption ringing in the house on 9 de Julio, because how could she imagine that handset bringing signs of Chile? Seven days in which she could have gone back, retraced her steps, returned to the place she never should have left. One red light, a simple slip-up, and that's it. Not his lungs, from all that nicotine, not even the exhaustion of his seventy-three years. Why him and not Leonora with her convalescence, which should've taken her out of the game ages ago? Ania doesn't believe in miracles. She thinks she should have asked Javier to travel through the phone cord or through some other aperture and come straight to Campana, then and there, through the electrical grid. Come rescue her, bring her back. She walks out of the café and heads down the street with the ice cream parlors. Ciao, Coletti, she hears someone say. She looks all around. Is it her they're talking to? She doesn't waste time finding out, time has cracked. She walks straight, no destination, straight.

At the train station she sits on a wooden bench to wait. Just as she waited a few hours ago on Nélida's little green floor, now she settles herself onto a wooden seat and finds the most comfortable position to await a train that no longer runs. She listens as the fire station's siren plays its twelve o'clock song. As shrill as the cicadas, as the old folks' laughter, as the sound of the train pealing in the wee hours. A whole town that shrieks, that never shuts up, despite the silence it pretends to transmit. To one side of the station, right in front of the newspaper stand, she sees a ceramic virgin, a vase with two fresh lilies and a message written on the marble in sky-blue letters: *Heavenly Mother of Campana, virgin of safe travels, may I reach my destination safely, today and on the following journey.* Further on, a bone-colored dog, scrawny, sleeps under the little wooden bench occupied by a cop. After a while the dog gets up, walks over to her and lies at her feet. It's not a rat-dog, like her father's. It's not her father, lying at her feet. It's a big stray, shattered by life. If ships came down the tracks, she'd climb aboard the first one that blew its horn. She'd threaten the captain with a knife or whatever she could find and force him to veer off his route downriver and head out to high seas. She'd climb aboard with the crew and the few passengers bound for any place of origin that wasn't hers. Ania knows that something, that everything, is broken. She thinks the best thing would be to walk to the hospital—Agustín's, Nélida's, hers—and pay the seventeen pesos an hour they charge to watch TV. And stay there a long time, spend the night watching images of some shipwreck on the other side of the world. Nothing in the world seems more real than that. But she rifles through her bag and can't find any money or weapons for self-defense. Better to get up and make the walk back down Avenida

139

Rocca. The stray follows her for a block and then grows bored and abandons her. In the plaza she stops beneath the jacaranda, in front of the monument to the immigrants. She feels the inscription means nothing to her. She didn't come like a wave behind the ocean; she simply crossed a mountain. "The only place for those who commit genocide is in jail," she once more reads on the wall. She tries to think about that, establish some connection, but her mind right now is a blank screen. She walks to Cecil's, despite the risk of bumping into Gariglio again. There aren't many people at this hour, it's almost dark. No sign of Gariglio, luckily. She looks for an empty table and takes a seat. On the floor, right under her table, she finds a red silk scarf. Blood red. She doesn't know why she does it, there's no time to process. Because she's cold, because it looks so soft, because it's been abandoned there on the floor. Lies: because it's almost the same as the one she gave her father for his birthday. It's obvious that somebody has forgotten it and will be back for it, but Ania doesn't think about that. It's not actually silk but some cheap imitation, yet she couldn't care less now that she's got it in her hand. A scarf standing in for another scarf, same story. She slips it into her bag and situates herself on the chair. Outside it starts to drizzle, the sky being torn up into little pieces. It's going to be a shitty fall. She never spent a fall in Campana, it was always summers: December to February, most of the time, then back with her father, to her homeland to start March together, alone, like the little two-member family, the self-sufficient nucleus they formed for years, until Leonora turned up. She's never even stolen a silk scarf before, she's never stolen. Ania calls the waiter the way she's always done—waiter! waiter!—no regard for manuals of good conduct. She wants to go back to being herself. She pulls a pencil out of her purse and takes a napkin from the dispenser on the table. She tries to plan what to do in the next hours. Ania wants to make a list, but isn't quite sure of what. She decides she must act, must go back. She can't put the decision off any longer: she has to return as quickly as she came. Not stand in for her father anymore but for herself. The side of herself that will remain here, without her entirely wanting it to. On the canvas of her mind the only thing she sees are images of a daughter holding vigil over a father in a hospital room. If things miraculously turn out okay, she'll ask the doctors to leave them alone and tell him everything. She doesn't know exactly what *everything* is, but she'll tell him everything. Even if she's talking to a vegetable and her words bounce around the air. If things turn out bad, she'll keep calm, behave the way an orphan or a widow does, and when the others are distracted, she'll kidnap him and run off with him to this side of the mountain. She'll bring him back in a little box, as if he were antique jewelry, one of Nélida's precious necklaces. And he'll finally be back with his people, his whole family. Now she looks in her purse, ready to pull out the trophy and cover her face with the red silk scarf. Red mourning, befitting for the daughter of an elusive father. But just at that moment, a man wearing an anguished expression walks into Cecil's and begins snooping around the tables. It's quite clear that he's looking for the scarf. Ania hears him speak to the barman. Now, together, they're searching every table. They ask for permission to look under her feet. What's more, now Ania herself joins the search for the fake silk scarf. But she's unwilling to hand over her booty, how else is she supposed to keep vigil over her father? She can't abandon him just when she got him back. She excuses herself and goes to the bathroom. Once alone in the restroom she takes the scarf out of her bag, covers half of her face with it (leaving her eyes uncovered) and finally looks in the mirror after a week of not seeing herself. Relief at still existing. Anguish at having lost him.

THE ITALIAN IMMIGRANT'S MANUAL (1913)

Passport. Have you never seen what a passport looks like? I will describe it for you. It is a printed booklet comprised of 20 pages. The first has the royal coat of arms, bears the King's name at the top, and contains the passport holder's basic information, that is, the emigrant's first and last names, parentage, place of birth, profession and place of residence in Italy. On the second page come his personal details, that is, height, shape of forehead, nose and mouth, color of his face, moustache and beard if he has them, any visible characteristics such as scars, defects, etc. This page also contains the emigrant's signature, providing he knows how to write.

In that night's dream, Ania is traveling across the sea in search of her father's remains. The ocean, below, strikes her as a biographical accident. At seventy-three, the man has fled Chile and landed in the Piedmont of his parentage. But with such bad luck that now he is a body rather than alive. People call them *remains*, as if they were leftover breadcrumbs. Ania travels light, her life fits in a carry-on. The red silk scarf (which in typical dream-distortion is more pinkish: blood diluted in water), the black sweatshirt, her jeans, a little bamboo hat to protect herself from the sun, her sleeping pills in a little transparent pillbox. And her passport, which she has to show at the border: Nélida Damilano. Registration no.: 1,807,740. Height: 166cm. Skin color: white. Hair: brown. Nose: straight. Eyes: brown. Mouth: medium. Ears: small. Then: fledge, cross the ocean, bring back her father.

Where were you?, Claudia asks on the other end of the line. Why weren't you answering? I thought you'd gone back to Chile. Ania doesn't know how to respond. She listens to her cousin's lecture with her tail between her legs. There's an interested party, someone who wants to buy the houses, both houses. Can you imagine, little cousin? The whole of 9 de Julio, patio, rotted grapes, all of it. It's incredible. No clue whether the guy wants to demolish them or refurbish them. But he wants them, can you imagine? We have to set a day for the viewing. Do you want me to be there too, to show the houses? I've been calling you for a thousand days and you don't answer the phone. We almost lost the buyer, where were you? You there, little cousin? Yes, little cousin's here, but she has no voice. *Crack.* After a struggle, something comes out of her mouth. Something Claudia wasn't expecting. It's true, Ania wasn't expecting it either: she didn't cross the mountain for this. Right, she says, it's like my head was cracked open. A bright red-hot wound deep, deep inside. The words resound like an echo on the other end of the line.

THE ITALIAN IMMIGRANT'S MANUAL (1913)

Behavior. And now that I've given you the most indispensable information required to successfully confront the place to which you are about to transplant your existence, I would like to tell you a few other things about the way to behave.

The girl is packing her case at her grandparents' house and Agustín is striking typewriter keys in time to a tedium that's not quite that of the provinces but one much deeper inside, less recognizable. Maybe tedium isn't the right word for what he feels. He abandons his typing exercise, crosses the patio and raps on the door next door. Excuse me, he says, I'm here to say goodbye. The grandparents are having breakfast at the dining room table. They're steeping maté and waiting for the girl with croissants, sweet potato paste, and cheese. And there's a glass of milk for her, since they know she hates maté. They're waiting for her to come down with her case. Her father has gone to run errands, tune up the Citroën, buy a few things for the drive back to Chile. The grandparents invite Agustín to join them. Would you like a maté, Tinito? No, no, I just came to say goodbye, he says. And remains standing in one corner, waiting for Chilenita's figure to appear at the top of the attic stairs. When he sees her coming down, it doesn't occur to him to help her with her luggage. His eyes bore into her, trying to retain her, to learn her face by heart. He looks hard at the bandage on her head, the white gauze specked with small red dots. Her wound is alive, Agustín thinks. Chilenita's blood has more life in it than I do. His body does not respond, he imagines never seeing her again. The girl has a little bamboo hat in one hand. To hide the bandage, no doubt. She has to take him with her, not leave him alone in this rusty old town. Please, please. Suddenly Agustín feels like he can't breathe. He asks if he can open the patio window. The grandparents ask him if he's hot. I just want to see the sky, he says. As if he hadn't just come in from outside or had never seen that celestial vault he now so urgently needs. The grandparents, however, take no notice. So he opens the window and looks out: cotton-ball clouds and a sun like a splinter jabbing into his eyes. Way up there, he thinks, that's where real life takes place. He closes the window, looks at the girl for the last time. It strikes him that come next summer he'll be gone and they'll still be having breakfast at that table, and splinters of sun will filter in through the window and prick their skin, and they will still be there. The maté, the splinters, the sun.

OMISSIONS AND ERRORS: On finishing
a document do not pull it from the
typewrinter without having first read it
over carefully, to insure there are no
omissions or reeros.This way you avoid the
inconvineince of having to reinsert the
sheet of paper (. . .) Typing on carbon
paper is when the greatest precaustions
must be taken, givent hat any erros made
on the original will,logically, also be
made on each of the copies. In this case,
you ust simply slip a piece of paper
between the carbon paper and the regular
paper, so the pressure exserted by the
eraser does not go through to the texts.

Ania repacks Nélida and Agustín's things just as she found them, back in the same box, except the typing notebooks. She takes the first one, the one from 1970, and slips it into her carry-on. Once everything is all ready, she hangs the family photos back on the wall. The only one she keeps is the portrait of her father. It hardly fits into her bag, but she manages to take it back with her. For the last time, she walks through every corner of 9 de Julio: her grandparents' room, the attic, her father's old room, the shared patio, the ramshackle grape arbor, the weeds out back, Nélida's room in the other house, Agustín's little alcove. Then she leaves a place she'll never see again. Out on the street Ania looks in the branches of the orange tree to see if she can spot a lone nest, but the birds are far away or no longer nest there. No fruit on the branches or the ground either. A sterile tree, a city emptying out. At that moment she recalls something she once read in her father's encyclopedia about sparrows being exterminated in China, in the late fifties. The Party decreed the birds a plague, said they ate the stored grain and produced great losses for the economy. And ordered the citizens to kill at least three sparrows a day. The Chinese, disciplined or fearful, didn't sleep until they'd hunted down every last bird in sight. And yet the sparrows ate not only grain crops but also insects. So the birds were no more, but the locusts arrived and that plague was relentless: it decimated crops and left the country in poverty. Cities with no birds, abandoned nests. With that image in mind, Ania walks to the bus that will take her to the capital to catch a plane back. She sees no one on the streets. As if everyone had been forced to flee and abandoned everything half-done, the city half-existing. Panic in paradise, she thinks. And she wants to laugh, but the laugh won't come. What does come is a thought about the near future. She thinks that in a few hours she will no longer be herself. She'll be a woman who has seen her father. She'd like to move twenty or thirty spaces back on the gameboard and be climbing into the Citroën for the return trip right now, copiloting the route with the man who brought her into the world. Puffy clouds, a breeze, the straight line of the road, the plains sucking them along, the sight of the mountains, the ascent. But the script has direct cuts, not fade-ins, and she submits to the dizzying speed of the scenes that follow. Once on the plane, she looks out the window and has the sense she's searching the air for something. The panic she feels at flying hasn't changed from when she was ten, fifteen, twenty years old. But now has the impression that the glimmering sun is keeping her safe. A velvety light brings things into focus, the little valleys, the hills, the peaks, the snow stretching across the summits. If she adjusts her gaze, she can touch the hills with her eyes. The plane judders. She knows the mountain is willing to receive her, with its yawning canyons. For her to land on rocky ground and build a provisional nest, far from the meekness of humanity. To stay and live amid the moss that breathes up at that altitude, amid the hardy brush. With the falkins and the snells. Suddenly it strikes her that the source of her problems is that she doesn't have a garden. Ania thinks watering a garden by night must be like rescuing a songless bird or crossing an ocean or furiously striking typewriter keys. And that with no garden and no birds and no keyboard or open seas where she can rinse off her mind, it all becomes so improbable. But she's certain, very certain, that in the near future, when all this is over, she'll have a garden and she'll water it with care. Like it was a little field out in the country, a small plot free of memories and blood. She'll use the touch system to water it, like it was a faint heart, with the meticulousness of a typist. And some nights she'll think she can hear the call of a bowerbird or the voice of her father. A sound that will seep into her head and keep her awake. And she'll get up in the night and arrange the hose and turn on the faucet and let the water flow into the tufts of grass and form a puddle that, drop by drop, will create the contours of her very own pond.

ACKNOWLEDGMENTS

All the thanks in the world to David Ponce, Juana Inés Casas, Andrea Palet, Lorena Amaro, Diego Zúñiga, Galo Ghigliotto, Alejandro Zambra, Cristian Geisse, Aníbal Gatica, Tania Lagos, Andrea Montejo and Paula Canal, who read the sprouts, branches and/or multiple versions of this book. My thanks, too, to Franca, Elsa, Nina, Franco, Luciano and the rest of the Piedmont clan, who opened furrows to memory and imagination. Thank you to Maria Nicola for suggesting other possible routes and welcoming me into her lair. Thank you to Vanina, who listened and was always there. Thank you to my father, of course: without him, this novel would not exist. And my greatest thanks to Norberto Lombardi, the last member of the tribe, for accompanying me to the end on a search as obsessive as it was memorable.

ALEJANDRA COSTAMAGNA was born in Santiago, Chile, in 1970. She is the author of four novels, four collections of short stories, and an anthology of newspaper columns. Her work has been translated into Italian, Korean and French, and since 2010, she has been a member of the editorial committee for the Chilean independent publishing house Cuneta. She lives in Santiago de Chile. *The Touch System* is her first novel to appear in English, and was a finalist for the 2018 Herralde Prize.

LISA DILLMAN translates from Spanish and teaches in the Department of Spanish and Portuguese at Emory University. Some of her recent translations include *Such Small Hands*, *The Right Intention,* and *A Luminous Republic* by Andrés Barba, *A Silent Fury* by Yuri Herrera, and *The Bitch* by Pilar Quintana, which was a finalist for the National Book Award. She lives in Decatur, GA.